MARVEL AVENGERS INFINITY WAR

THE COSMIC QUEST

VOLUME ONE: BEGINNING

BRANDON T. SNIDER

LITTLE, BROWN AND COMPANY

New York   Boston

marvelkids.com

© 2018 MARVEL

Cover design by Ching N. Chan. Cover illustration by Matt Taylor.

Little, Brown and Company
Hachette Book Group
1290 Avenue of the Americas, New York, NY 10104
Visit us at LBYR.com
marvelkids.com

First Edition: April 2018

Little, Brown and Company is a division of Hachette Book Group, Inc.
The Little, Brown name and logo are trademarks of Hachette Book Group, Inc.

The publisher is not responsible for websites (or their content) that are not owned by the publisher.

Library of Congress Control Number 2018931204

ISBNs: 978-0-316-48273-8 (paper over board), 978-0-316-48259-2 (ebook)

Printed in the United States of America

LSC-C

10 9 8 7 6 5 4 3 2 1

CONTENTS

FOREWORD

In the beginning, six singularities floated in the nothingness. They were powerful, but they were shapeless. When life emerged, thundering into existence, these six extraordinary things were forged into tangible pieces of rock. *The Infinity Stones.* Each one became the embodiment of a unique aspect of the universe itself—*Space, Time, Mind, Reality, Power,* and *Soul.* They were scattered across the cosmos and fell into the hands of powerful beings, who used them to dominate entire civilizations. Individually, the Infinity Stones have been wielded by many, but no one has dared to accumulate them all.

Until now.

CHAPTER 1

"Carina!" the Collector shouted. "Come here right now!" His hoarse voice echoed through the museum. He'd just woken up from a very irritating dream after falling asleep at his worktable. *Again*. It had been a long week. The Collector had been in the middle of recording his memoirs when he dozed off. These days, reliving his own stories in his head, over and over again, bored him to death. A girl shuffled into the room. She was tall, bald, and thin. Like most Zoobaazian females, her royal-blue skin was covered with small, shimmering scales. She wore a narrow silver frock, which hugged her body tightly and prevented her from moving easily. She often felt as if she were trapped in a cocoon. The Collector refused to let her wear anything else. Realizing she'd upset her master, the young woman grimaced and braced herself for a scolding.

"I told you to make sure I stayed awake." The Collector sighed. "Is it too much to ask that you follow directions?"

"My deepest apologies, sir," the girl said. Her big red eyes blinked rapidly. She was also half blind. "Since you hadn't been sleeping well, I thought it best to leave you be."

"You *thought*?" the Collector asked, aghast. "I don't pay you to *think*."

"You don't pay me at all, sir," the slave responded. "But that's okay! I'm happy to serve you." The girl hadn't eaten all day, which wasn't unusual for her—being overworked and without any personal time. This made her light-headed and unfocused, which she tried to hide. "I do have a bit of good news to share. While you were resting, I watered the museum's flora. Some of the more exotic plants were in desperate need of nutrition. Without proper care, they'll wither and—"

"*Die?* I know that," he grumbled. "You don't

think I know that?" He slammed his fist down on the table. Napping always made him cranky.

"Of course, sir. I'm so foolish. Again, allow me to offer my sincerest of apologies," the slave girl said with a bow. "Also, I must point out, yet again, my name isn't Carina. It's *Keelan*."

The Collector stared at her for a moment. He knew her name, but it didn't matter. To him, she was just a slave. Her only purpose was to serve. "I'll call you whatever I want to call you," he said dismissively, rubbing his eyes. "Don't correct me again."

Keelan's eyes narrowed. She formed a pained, humble smile. "Did you have another of your bad dreams, sir?" she asked.

"I told you to never speak of my dreams!" the Collector shouted. He touched the side of his face and realized he'd drooled all over himself. Embarrassed, he quickly used the back of his hand to wipe it away. "Don't look at me!" He reached into his cloak pocket and pulled out a handheld mirror. He held it up to his face and glared at his reflection. His skin was sallow, his eyes sunken. The once-white fur trim on his crimson cloak was grimy. He had become a shell of his former self.

"I'm only trying to help, sir. That's all I wish to do," Keelan said. Her tone was now pleasant and perky, her eyes bright. "How can I be of service, my great and powerful master?"

"Fetch me a drink, then leave me alone so that I may continue documenting my existence," he said, shooing away Keelan with the flick of his wrist. The girl nodded and quickly walked away, the sound of her shoes tapping against the floor in a way the Collector found upsetting. Was this girl *intentionally* trying to drive him crazy?

The Collector pushed himself up from his workbench with great effort and glanced around his formerly impressive museum. It was no longer the grand menagerie he'd built for himself. It had become a disaster. A careless *incident* had destroyed his home and changed everything in the process. This filled him with great sadness and anger. He looked toward the ceiling and winced.

It was black with soot and crumbling to pieces. Frayed cables dangled from above. Small piles of debris were scattered across the floor. Tubes once filled with strange liquids were bone-dry and cracking.

The armory? Looted. The galaxy's most menacing weapons gone.

The Collector's extraordinary zoo? Demolished. Creatures from unknown worlds either destroyed or escaped.

Everything was in a state of disrepair. It was all too much. He shook off the pain and sat back down. There was work to be done. Perhaps he could refocus if he started over from the beginning.

The Collector looked at the hexagonal disk on his workbench and tapped it gently. The sound of his own voice filled the museum. It instantly comforted him.

"My name is Taneleer Tivan. Some think me to be eccentric. I can see that. But one thing is for certain—I'm not a good person. Nor do I seek to be one. What I am is a survivor. I've lived a very long time and have seen the universe take many shapes. Technically, I could be ruling over all of existence if that's what I wished. I've put in the time and energy. I have the conviction. But it simply doesn't hold my interest. The power I crave comes from amassing the galaxy's most sought-after items. This has been my greatest enterprise. I've possessed an incredible menagerie of relics and creatures, culled from the far reaches of space. Unique antiques. Strange alien beings. Items of great curiosity. I've trafficked in all these things. They are my currency. If they are or were important to the cosmos, they are important to me. Some people are fulfilled by relationships and the connections they build with the beings around them. I am not one of those people. I desire *things*. They give me life. Things define my existence. Things infuse my world with meaning. Without them, I have no purpose. Things are what we leave behind. They contain our stories. They are our legacy. Living creatures always disappoint, but things, if preserved and cared for, last forever. That's why

I acquire them. This is why I'm known as the Collector."

He stopped the recording. Keelan entered the room carrying a large tray upon which sat a single glass of Phelch Juice. It was the Collector's favorite refreshment, made from a race of sentient vegetables. He swiped the glass from the tray and gulped it down like someone who'd gone days without drink. "Was that too reflective? Too self-indulgent?" he asked, eyeing his slave. "Tell me the truth."

Keelan froze. Whenever her master asked for the truth, her body tensed. It always felt like a trick question. She'd learned to keep a handful of diplomatic responses at the ready. "I didn't think it polite to listen," she said.

"Good girl," the Collector replied. She'd passed his test. "My nightmares are prophetic, you know. I'm convinced. In them, I see myself swallowed by cosmic forces. That's why I've chosen to chronicle my existence using one of these Memory Disks. It will serve as my private time capsule. Something to preserve my legacy so the universe will always remember me. I've put all kinds of stories and musings into this impenetrable little recording device." He tapped the hexagonal disk, turning it off. "I'm trying to find a balance of *power* and *intrigue*. I can't tell if my introduction covers all the bases. I've dictated it more than ten times, but I'm not sure if it captures the full breadth of my magnificence just yet." He rose from his work-bench once more and began pacing. That always helped him think. Or so he thought.

Keelan's eyes followed the Collector as he darted through rows of vacant cases and exhibits, which was no simple task—the cavernous space was so dark these days that it was difficult to make out much beyond vague, shadowy shapes.

"May I help you look for something?" she asked.

He ignored the question. He wasn't looking for something he had, he was thinking about something he'd lost. Or many somethings. The sight of empty cages, one after the other, filled him with regret. He moved his hand back and forth across their rusty bars, sighing. Through his organization, the Tivan Group, the Collector had assembled the rarest pieces of exotica in the cosmos. Aliens from every system had lined up to sell him recovered artifacts, strange beasts, and whatever else they thought he might like. If the Collector wanted something, he got it. He paid top dollar, too, which had made him a respected figure in the community. Though he wasn't always fond of his location, Knowhere provided him access to a variety of groups. He'd become part of an underground network of traders and merchants. Some of them were less than desirable, but that was an expected part of the business. He'd learned how to work with them, setting up shop on a backwater mining colony inside the severed head of a godly being.

After *the incident*, his standing had changed. Many former associates considered him a joke. No one wanted to deal with a washed-up has-been. Trying to rebuild his museum had depleted his financial resources. He was on the verge of bankruptcy, though that didn't stop him from attempting to acquire new items. The Collector always had a trick up his sleeve.

"Your museum will reach great heights once again," Keelan said. "I just know it!"

Keelan's relentlessly positive attitude annoyed him. He grabbed a bar of an empty cage and squeezed as tightly as he could. The force of his grip made his entire body tremble. "Indeed, it shall," the Collector grumbled. *She has no idea what I've been through*, he thought. *She has no idea the loss I've suffered. I'd built my menagerie into a thing of beauty, and in the blink of an eye, a brainless and insolent act destroyed millennia's worth of my hard work. The things that gave my life meaning are either lost or broken beyond repair. I've been left with barely anything to show for it, and here she is smiling at me like an imbecile!* He released his grip. His anger lifted, if only for a moment. "I'm bored with wallowing. I must refocus on the task at hand. I want a story, Keelan. Uplift me. A happy tale of your youth on Zoobaaz, perhaps?

Anything to yank me out of this pathetic haze."

Keelan stood silently for a moment, lost in thought, then suddenly her face brightened. "I believe I have just the thing," she said. "My family were simple folk, you see. Farmers. We lived far from the city and didn't have much else apart from one another. That was all we needed, really. My parents raised my sister and me to be strong and proud. Smart, too! I struggled with my studies. My brain can get fuzzy sometimes, as you know. At the end of a long school day, I used to play in the fields. It brought us such joy to feel so free. Oh, and the rain! We loved the rain. It filled the gully to the top, and we'd swim till our arms were tired." Keelan sniffled. She'd recently heard that Zoobaaz had been devastated by a mysterious force, but there were no other details. Her family was missing. Thinking about what might've happened to them caused her great pain. "I miss them all so much. Every day I think of them. *Every. Day.*" Tears burst from her eyes.

The Collector twiddled his fingers in the air to

make it all stop. "No, no, no," he said, shaking his head. "End this story. There's to be no rambling and definitely no *weeping* in the museum."

Keelan wiped her tears and took a deep breath. Her face cleared itself of all emotion. "Understood, sir." She stared at her master, awaiting instruction.

The Collector felt uncomfortable. He spotted a small vat of bubbling orange ooze and walked over to it. "I think it's time for an inspection," he said, placing his finger on the edge of the vat. He slowly dragged his fingertip along the edge, never breaking eye contact with Keelan. "Dusty," he whispered. "What do you have to say for yourself?"

Keelan did her best to remain composed. "Apologies again, sir," she began. "It can be difficult to keep your beautiful museum as pristine as you require it to be. You see, your esteemed guests—their clothing is covered in tiny specks that gather in the air and fall upon this place without our seeing. These traveled men and women—wanderers, explorers of great station—they bring with them space particles. Our very universe attaches itself to them and—"

"I didn't ask for a history of dust," the Collector growled, cutting her off. "Clean this place. Top to bottom. When you've finished, I'll give you another task. Oh, and these wanderers you speak of? They're thieves, brigands, and desperate beings who would sell their families for the smallest measure of wealth. Don't mistake them for heroes. I deal with them because I *have* to, not because I want to. Never forget that."

Keelan's eyelids fluttered. She was smiling, though she didn't look happy. "Yes, Collector," she said with a bow and a curtsy. "I shall return in a moment."

As Keelan shuffled away, the Collector returned to his workbench. Scattered on its surface were tools, maps, and other items in various states of disrepair. Gazing at it all, and frustrated with his memoirs, he felt the need to direct his attention to his *other* life's work: the Infinity Stones. He coveted *them* above all else. They were extraordinary things that defied belief. Born at the beginning of existence and infused with energy few had the power to wield.

The red *Reality Stone* transformed existence at will.

The yellow *Mind Stone* granted near-limitless mental abilities.

The blue *Space Stone* gave its wielder the ability to travel through the cosmos almost immediately.

The green *Time Stone* allowed one to play with time itself.

The purple *Power Stone* endowed its wielder with cosmic strength, durability, and the ability to project energy blasts.

And the orange *Soul Stone*'s potential remained a mystery....

Individually, they were impressive. Together, they were unstoppable. He desired them more than anything else. At one time, acquiring them was his only mission. Then things changed. When tragedy struck, only his quest for the Stones gave him comfort. The Infinity Stones were oh so *elusive*. Chasing after them was part of the fun.

"Keelan!" he exclaimed. "Have you heard anything?" His vague question was meant as another test. He wanted to see if his slave knew what he was talking about without his being specific. He assumed she would. She always did. Despite her simple mind, Keelan was often perceptive.

Keelan scurried into the room, her arms full of cleaning products. She looked at the Collector, expecting him to clarify his question. He just smiled. Beads of sweat soon appeared on Keelan's forehead as she trembled with confusion. "I, um, well, I don't know," she stumbled. "What was it I was supposed to be listening for, sir? Forgive me for asking. I know I'm to keep track of all your desires and requests, but there are so many. Would you permit me to look to my journals for the answer?"

"What would a diary tell you that could possibly be helpful?" the Collector barked.

"Oh no. I do not keep diaries. I would never

share my personal thoughts in such a manner. I keep journals. And they are dedicated to you, dear Collector. I make note of all your likes, dislikes, and interests. Because your queries are fairly cyclical, I've put them into an estimated timetable. That way I can be prepared with an acceptable answer when prompted."

"How innovative and also incredibly odd," remarked the Collector.

"It's very helpful!" Keelan grinned.

"And yet now, at this pivotal moment, you have *nothing*?"

Keelan was speechless. Her master's question hung in the air. She was desperate to maintain the happy facade despite her disappointment.

"The Infinity Stones," the Collector whispered. "Have you heard anything of their whereabouts?"

Keelan sighed with relief before a grave look took over her face. "There's been no change in their status, sir," she stated firmly. "No credible leads at this time." She was always careful when speaking about the Infinity Stones. The Collector talked to her about them rarely, if ever. Mostly after he'd had his nightly elixirs. His passion for them scared her. If she were to steer him in the wrong direction, he'd never forgive her. Or worse.

"Very well," the Collector said. He felt immediately anxious. "When was the last time you took inventory, Keelan?"

"This morning," she answered. "As is my daily routine."

"Take it again," he commanded.

Keelan nodded and dashed away, cleaning supplies left in a heap on the ground.

The Collector retired to his study and settled into his chair. It was a worn old thing. Big by any standard. Red velvet cushions, flattened over time. The odd stain or two. It was one of his very first purchases. He liked it because it resembled a throne, not because it possessed any special qualities. He simply liked the way it made him feel.

He'd hoped for better news about the Infinity Stones, but he had gotten what he'd expected.

There was a time when the galaxy's snitches and sneaks lined up around the corner to share hot tips about the Stones and their whereabouts. Many were dead ends, but every so often, there was a kernel of good news. If a lead produced a credible result, its deliverer was paid handsomely. That was when the Collector had funds. Now people took their information elsewhere, but he'd always maintained contact with underworld figures in the know. He'd been forced to sell many of his remaining possessions at a low cost to keep his home. Items he never dreamed he would part with, traded for scraps. It was how he survived. He hadn't given up on possessing the Infinity Stones just yet, but he needed time. He needed resources. He needed money.

The Collector once briefly considered selling the Xandarian Boulder-Crusher he kept in the basement but eventually decided against it. It was a rare find. One of the last of its kind. He didn't want to lose it despite the fact that a giant snake creature was worth a lot of money on the black market. He was convinced there were other ways to return his museum to greatness—he simply hadn't found them yet.

For the time being, he tried his best to focus on what he *had*, not what he wanted.

The Collector had come into possession of the Reality Stone quite naturally and without fanfare. Two of Asgard's famous warriors, Sif and Volstagg, entrusted it to him after a nasty Dark Elf incident forced them to seek a new place to store the dangerous item. The Asgardians believed the Reality Stone, housed inside a containment unit known as the Aether, would be safe amid the Collector's menagerie. And it was—for a time. The Collector grew obsessed with the Aether's raw power, staring at the swirling red energy for hours on end. He'd become preoccupied with learning its secrets and wondered how he might wield such a thing if given the chance. Thus far, a proper opportunity to unleash the Aether had eluded him. For a variety of reasons.

CRASH!

"Master!" Keelan cried out. Her scream was unsettling. "Help! Help, help, help!" She raced through the museum, chasing after something.

The Collector sat still as a slithering, log-size tentacle wriggled underneath his chair. It seemed to be looking for a place to hide. Keelan rushed into the room and thwapped the creature's hindquarters with a broom in an attempt to corral it. *"Back away!"* the Collector barked. He cleared Keelan from his space, reached under his chair, and grabbed the tentacle with force. It writhed in pain as he slowly squeezed it into submission, his hand soaked through with purple ooze. Keelan was both impressed and disturbed. "Would you mind fetching that for me, dear?" the Collector asked, pointing to a cube-shaped case on a shelf nearby. Keelan did as she was told, shuddering as her master shoved the tentacle into the cube and locked it inside. Keelan grabbed a handful of towels and dried her master's slime-covered hand.

"Keelan, have a seat," the Collector said softly.

He offered her a minuscule stool, a mere quarter of her size. He'd recovered it from a troll colony once upon a time. Keelan's oversize frame caused the stool to creak as she sat down. "Would you mind doing me a favor, dear?" the Collector asked. He took a long, deep breath before speaking again. "Explain to me, if you don't mind, why I just had to wrangle a runaway tentacle."

"I'd just started doing inventory as you had instructed," she began. "I figured it was a good idea to count the sentient tentacles first. Since their terrarium is so large, they tend to hide. I can never really see how many are inside."

"But, Keelan, precious, we possess only one sentient tentacle. You *accidentally* released the other two from captivity over a week ago. Do you not recall?"

Keelan's mouth dropped. "Oh yes," she said softly. "I suppose I forgot about that."

"Continue," the Collector said softly.

"I—I leaned on the glass, and the terrarium

shattered, causing the tentacle to escape through the museum," Keelan said. It looked as if she was about to cry. Then her expression changed. "But a miracle happened! You, the Collector, keeper of the universe's wonders, heroically retrieved it! You tamed the beast with your bare hands, which I gratefully cleaned upon your victory. I truly marvel at your strength, sir. You showed the creature great might. It was glorious to behold."

Keelan's compliments often could cool the Collector's boiling fury. As was the case in this instance. He found her funny and charming in a strange way he couldn't quite identify. "Thank you," he said, placing the boxed tentacle on a shelf. As he did so, he noticed a treasure was missing. "Where is my Dotaki skull?!" he exclaimed.

"I—I—" Keelan stammered. "It was there this morning when I did the first inventory of the day. I know it was. I remember distinctly."

"An enormous black skull covered in spikes doesn't just get up and walk away!" the Collector shouted. "Show me the security footage. *Now.*"

Keelan trembled with fear.

"Tell me you installed the security system so I may monitor the activities within my museum whenever the need arises, dear, sweet Keelan."

"I forgot," she said, her voice tiny and shaking.

Instead of throwing something, the Collector, instead, deflated. Her behavior exhausted him. He lumbered back over to his chair and collapsed into it, unable to understand how such an oversight could have occurred. *Is it my destiny to be saddled with incompetent slaves for my remaining days? Is this my punishment for leading a life of malcontent?* he wondered.

Keelan, in the meantime, was silent. She relied on the Collector to give her purpose, even when that purpose slipped her mind. The Collector had a new idea. *Perhaps a mission will give my Keelan renewed purpose and allow her to become the slave I need her to be*, he thought.

"Keelan, you are to find the thief who took the

Dotaki skull, and you are to bring him before me. Use all your resources. Countless beings in this universe would revel in my shame and defeat. Who'd do anything to prevent me from returning to my perch atop the cosmic food chain. Whoever pilfered this item will pay with their life. That, I can promise. Now go. Be gone. And know this—if you do not accomplish this task, you, Keelan, will suffer the consequences. Do you understand?"

Keelan nodded. Tears welled in her eyes. For a brief moment, the Collector saw a despair that he couldn't address. He didn't think it was appropriate. She was a slave, and he was her master. Sympathy would give her power over him, and that just wouldn't do.

"I will find the culprit and bring him before you so that he can be punished accordingly," Keelan said firmly, swallowing her urge to break down. "And I thank you for the opportunity to do so."

"You're a good girl, Keelan," the Collector said. "Not *always*, but enough of the time that I don't wake up each morning wanting to pawn you off on someone else."

"Uh-oh." Keelan gulped. She'd just remembered something important. "Glorious and wise Collector, I've made another grave oversight the likes of which I may never forgive myself for. You see, sir, you're expected at Pungo's Pawnshop."

"When?" the Collector asked softly.

Keelan glanced up at the clock and frowned. "Now."

The Collector's body tensed as he gripped the sides of his chair. Without a word, he rose from his seat and straightened his tunic. He nodded at Keelan, tossed his cloak over his shoulder, and headed out the door to his appointment.

CHAPTER 2

Pungo's Pawnshop was a mystery to the average citizens of Knowhere. It was on a side street, down an alley, behind a butcher shop, next to a garbage-incineration facility, inside a colony of living pods, at the end of a long corridor on the third floor. There was no sign. There were barely any lights. Finding the place took work.

The Collector hated going there. Slogging through the streets to meet a lowlife like Pungo was embarrassing. It made him feel desperate. Pungo was a low-level player who had a habit of passing off trash as treasure, and yet the Collector regularly dealt with him now. He had to. Pungo often came through for him when no one else did. The Collector told himself he was doing what he had to do to take his menagerie to the next level. Besides, he hadn't left his museum in a while. A little air couldn't hurt.

Sadly, the air inside Pungo's was anything but fresh. The Collector held his nose as he entered the shop. The whole place smelled like cigars and wet towels. It was enough to make anyone sick. A stray beastie skittered across the Collector's toes, and he quickened his pace. He rushed past the front desk, through the gallery of broken blasters and alien jewelry, straight back to Pungo's office. Pungo had just received a batch of brand-new wares, among them an assortment of odd creatures, and he had called the Collector for a first look, an invitation that had almost been missed. But he was here now. And was hoping one of these new wares might be interesting enough to purchase.

Pungo's office was humid and cramped. A single yellow light hung from the middle of the ceiling. He sat at an old-style desk covered with critters and crumbs. The area behind him was blocked by a curtain and off-limits to most buyers.

That's where he kept the good stuff. Luckily, the Collector wasn't most buyers.

Pungo himself was a strange sight to behold. His pink body was large and gelatinous, like a fleshy blob that had slowly deteriorated over time. He moved like a slug, his legs folded up underneath his body. His arms reminded the Collector of tubes of meat, bursting out of their casings. A tiny bowler hat sat atop Pungo's pasty, rotund head. He wore an outdated headset. His floor-length, stringy black hair was soaked with grease, which dripped onto the moldy tiles below.

He was annoyed by the Collector's lack of punctuality. "Yer late," Pungo said with a wheeze.

"My slave misinformed me of our meeting time," the Collector said, taking a seat.

Pungo smiled. "*Ahhh.* So how is Keelan workin' out dese days?" he asked.

The Collector took a moment to consider his response. "She's worth every unit. Perhaps you want to show me a newer, better model slave?"

he asked, motioning to the curtain behind Pungo. "I'm always looking."

"Patience, my friend," Pungo said. He coughed for a minute straight. His mouth remained wide open the entire time. Green mucus flew in all directions.

"*Hmmmm*. Yes. *Friend,*" the Collector sighed, resisting the urge to pull out a handkerchief and dab at his face.

A small rodent scrambled across Pungo's desk. He grabbed it viciously and tossed the creature into his mouth, swallowing it whole. "Too salty," he complained. "You want one? I got more in my drawer. Ah but, now that I think about it, those are pretty old. Probably too chewy. I could fry 'em, though, if yer interested."

The Collector became agitated. "You told me you had items you wanted to show me. I'm here to see them, and my time is valuable."

Pungo chuckled to himself. "You don't like comin' out of your hole anymore, do ya? I get it.

I'm the same way. Mostly because I can't really move. Don't worry, once the other buyer gets here, we'll get dis show on the road. Then you can be on your way."

Another buyer?! the Collector thought, furious. He hated haggling and despised Pungo for pitting him against someone else. Haggling was for peasants. Collectors *bid*.

Pungo's office door swung open. His eyes lit up with anticipation. The second buyer had arrived.

"Well, well, well," a familiar voice muttered. "What an interesting little surprise."

———

As the Collector turned to greet the buyer, he felt a shiver run through his body. He recognized the voice. It belonged to his estranged brother, En Dwi Gast, the Grandmaster. The two of them stared at each other in silence. It had been a long time since they'd seen each other in person. The Grandmaster was dressed in his usual luxurious garb. A decadent golden robe. Designer sandals. Comfortable but clearly impeccably made pants.

He carried with him an over-the-shoulder satchel. But upon looking closer, the Collector noticed the Grandmaster wasn't without some wear and tear. His hair was whiter than usual. His eyes looked swollen, his body slightly gaunt. The Collector never thought his brother was that attractive to begin with, but now he appeared tired and haggard, as though he'd been through an intense experience.

"You look...*well*, En Dwi." His brother smirked.

"You two know each other?" asked Pungo.

The Collector's eyes narrowed. "You could say that."

"Don't be coy, Tivan!" the Grandmaster said, plopping into a chair and scooting over next to his annoyed brother. "He's just being shy, Pungo. Tivan and I are brothers, you see. Dear, *dear* brothers." The Grandmaster pointed to the blue streak running down the Collector's chin. "This mark means we're family. Isn't that clever?" His finger slowly and methodically inched closer to his brother's face. As it was about to make contact, the Grandmaster swiped it away and pointed to his own grinning face. "I've got one, too. But don't go mistaking us for twins." The Grandmaster's smile grew wider as he moved his face close to the Collector's and stared at him. It was a scare tactic meant to make him feel uncomfortable. It worked. The Collector was thrown off guard. He wasn't prepared for this encounter, yet the Grandmaster seemed entirely unfazed. Had he known that the Collector would be here today? Before he could ask the question, a small, stinky beast galloped into the room and perched itself at the Grandmaster's feet. "Go *away*, Spord!" he exclaimed, batting the hairy creature on the head. "This *thing* is bonded to my scent. I won it in a bet. Spord was supposed to *protect* me, like a bodyguard, but all it seems to do is shed and whimper. Pungo, would you mind opening a small portal? Destination unknown, preferably."

Pungo did as he was told. He grabbed a clunky, old device from under his seat and smacked its sticky buttons with his plump fingers. A small, murky portal opened on the ground beside him. The Grandmaster fished a glowing white ball from his pocket. He showed it to Spord, who'd been slobbering all over the ground. "Fetch!" the Grandmaster said, tossing the ball through the portal. Spord leaped after it as the portal closed behind it. "Free at last!" the Grandmaster exclaimed, then turned his attention back to their host. "So, Pungo, you pig-nosed nothing, how the devil are you?"

"Can't complain," Pungo said. "Glad you could make the trek. I heard about what happened on Sakaar. It's a shame how those ungrateful cretins treated you. After everything you did for them!"

The Collector perked up. He wanted details. "What happened to my brother on Sakaar, Pungo?" he asked. "A fall from grace, perhaps? Do tell."

"Bahp, bahp, bahp! Now is not the time for stories. Pungo, you just keep your mouth shut, or I'll take every filthy thing you own by force, then I'll melt you and your family. Okay?" the

Grandmaster threatened, his tone unchanged and a small smile still on his face. "Oh, and was that a Shakuss Tusk I saw in the foyer? How much?"

"Um, ah, that's not fer sale," Pungo said with a nervous giggle.

BEEP! BEEP! BEEP!

Pungo's headset indicated a call was coming through. "A moment, please," he said, taking the call. The Collector and the Grandmaster sat quietly until the lingering silence became unbearable.

"What are you doing here, En Dwi?" the Collector asked. "Isn't a place like this beneath someone of your stature? Assuming you still have any stature."

The Grandmaster always appreciated a solid jab from his brother, especially since he hadn't heard one in so long. It made him miss their rivalry. "Coming to this overflowing toilet of a planetoid *is* beneath my stature. You are correct. However, I'm in need of a bodyguard. After a recent bit of trauma on Sakaar, I've found myself in need of added protection. Spord, sadly, has not proved to do the trick."

"Trauma?" the Collector questioned. "How terribly *dreadful*. You poor thing."

"I'm still standing, brother. Do not doubt it," corrected the Grandmaster. "A cosmic idol such as I requires defense. A burly escort. A muscle-headed guardian. Pungo has provided me with affordable options in the past, so I made an appointment. It was an extreme inconvenience to my very busy schedule, but I'm nothing if not adaptable."

The Grandmaster's declaration caused the Collector to release an involuntary and prolonged snicker. "Yes. *Adaptable*."

"And who's to say I wasn't also here to see *you*, *too*?" asked the Grandmaster. "I couldn't possibly pass up a chance to spend time with family, now could I?"

"Mmm," the Collector murmured.

"What does that even mean?!" exclaimed the Grandmaster. "What does *mmm* mean?!"

"It was but a *sound*, brother."

"Not coming from you, it wasn't."

"*Affordable options.* Unique choice of words."

"I meant to say *acceptable*! Why are *you* here? Looking to outbid me? I know you've tried in the past. We've dealt with the same brokers. I have ears everywhere. I know more about *you* than you might think."

Before the Collector could respond, Pungo finished his call and turned his attention back to his guests. "Sorry 'bout that. Family issues. M'boy is sick," he said, sifting through a stack of papers on his desk. He found a photograph and tossed it in front of his guests. In it, a stout, pig-nosed child frowned. "Little Gluddy. Isn't he great? Says he wants ta grow up and be jus' like his daddy."

"A stinking trash collector with a shop full of broken junk?" the Grandmaster scoffed. "Tell Gluddy to aim higher."

The Collector raised his hand in peace. "May we see your wares now, Pungo?" he asked. "I have other places to be."

Pungo reached behind him and yanked on a thick, dirty rope. The curtain went up, and the day's top three selections were revealed.

"Dis here is a G'Zara," Pungo said, presenting the first beast. The hunchbacked creature had enormous, piercing eyes and a mouth that couldn't close. His body was pale gray, covered in fuzz, with a long scar running from his neck to its waist. "The cool thing about dis guy is that his innards have been completely replaced. If ya think about it, it's like he's brand-new! Except the brain. That could use a tune-up. He's nonverbal but takes commands okay."

The G'Zara jolted himself back and forth as if having a seizure.

"He does that." Pungo said.

The creature reared back and expelled a chunky white substance that had apparently been brewing deep within his belly. Milky goo splattered across the floor. The stench made the Collector gag. Pungo waved the creature out the door and moved on to the next.

"Dis right here is a marvel of technology! Nuthin' gets past Ergon 450," he said, presenting a tall silver robot. "And to think, some idiot on Xandar was gonna throw dis guy away." Pungo used a long stick to press a button on the robot's back that triggered a deafening high-pitched sound. Streams of thick black smoke shot out of its mouth and eyes. "Abort! Abort!" Pungo shouted. He flipped a switch under his desk, activating a fan that pumped the smoke out of the room.

The Collector and the Grandmaster were visibly displeased. Pungo must have caught on to their facial expressions, because he chuckled nervously and rubbed his hands together. "What a day! Heh heh. I think you'll both really like what's up next," he said, unveiling the third and final item. It was a sleeping humanoid woman, covered head to toe in a black bodysuit. The brothers were quite intrigued. Pungo tossed a bucket of ice water on the woman, jolting her awake.

"Where am I? Who are you?" she demanded,

shivering. The woman took one look at her surroundings and made a break for it. She kicked Pungo in the face, smashed through a window with her fist, and jumped out to freedom.

The room was silent, its occupants speechless.

Mental note: Track down that female immediately, the Collector thought. *She'd be perfect for the menagerie.*

Pungo couldn't help but break the awkwardness with his babbling. "What else, what else? I got a Dotaki skull on its way soon. I hope. Fingers crossed."

The Collector shot up. "I'm *missing* a Dotaki skull," he blurted out.

A dribble of sweat formed on Pungo's upper lip. "I don't know a thing about dat," he said. "There's a bunch of 'em out there these days, you know. Not as rare as they used to be."

"Of course," the Collector said, lowering back into his seat, but still suspicious.

"Would you be interested in a Hadron Enforcer?

I got it secondhand. The thing is kind of glitchy. I'm willing to make a deal. If not, no worries. I'll pass it off on some poor dummy."

The Grandmaster had seen enough. "I came all the way here, and you show me these broken playthings?!" he shouted. "You told me you had *brutes*. You told me you had *monsters*. You told me you had beings that could *crush things with their bare hands*! You've wasted my time, Pungo, and I won't soon forget it."

"*WAIT!*" Pungo shouted. He pointed toward a crate in the corner. "Hand me that, would you, Tivan?" The Collector rolled his eyes before honoring the request. Pungo peeled the top off and removed two small boulders. "These just came in dis morning," he said. "They're Wishing Ores. Crack one. I'm tellin' you, you'll like what's inside. Promise."

"They are certainly exotic," the Collector said, eyeing the basic gray rock.

"Go ahead, Grandmaster," said Pungo. "Make a wish."

The Grandmaster grabbed one of the boulders and tossed it to the ground, splitting it in half. A tiny, lizard-like fairy emerged from inside. It spread its wings and flittered through the air doing loop-the-loops. The Collector was intrigued. "Oh my," he gasped.

The Grandmaster swatted the fairy onto the desk and smashed it with the palm of his hand. He carefully inspected the imp's orange guts. "Everyone knows a Wishing Ore fairy is filled with rainbow sparkles. *This* is a fake," he said, scooping up a handful of the brightly colored innards and wiping them across Pungo's face. "I should melt you for trying to sell me this garbage, swine boy, but seeing you covered with goop brings me a comparable amount of joy. Almost worth the trip."

The substance dripped from Pungo's chin onto his clothing, creating a significant wet spot. He was embarrassed and ashamed. "I'm sorry, Grandmaster. I didn't mean to trick you or nuthin'. The market is slow. Times are tough for everyone. You lost your whole business. I *know* you know what I'm talking about."

The Grandmaster's eyes widened. He knew exactly what Pungo was talking about, but his brother did not. "Mouth shut, fat man!" he yelled.

The Collector found his brother's reaction suspicious and filed it away in his brain for future reference. He understood his brother's frustrations; after all, he had come to Pungo's hoping to find something new and wonderful, too, but was left feeling drained by the entire interaction. It was time to call it a day and move on. "Pungo, do you or do you not have anything of real value?" he asked.

Pungo shook his head in anguish. "The only thing I got for you, Tivan, is a little somethin' about those pretty rocks I know you love so much. A rumor I ain't checked out yet," he muttered. "Heard there's an Infinity Stone floatin' around on Knowhere."

The Collector perked up immediately. "Go on," he said, his voice lilting.

"That's everything I got at the moment, or I would have told you first thing I seen ya," Pungo said. "I know you're into those funny rocks, Tivan. They're a little too crazy for me, but I'd find one for you if that's what you wanted. To make up for what happened when that other one blew up your place."

"I...don't...we need not discuss...*that*," the Collector stammered.

The Grandmaster took note of his brother's curious response and made a mental note to address it with him later. He'd heard rumors of the Collector's demise, but he hadn't put much stock in them. Now he wondered what was truth and what was fiction.

Pungo rubbed his belly. "All dis talk is makin' me hungry," he said.

"*Which* Infinity Stone?" the Collector persisted. "Out with it."

"Ah, um, well, ya know, I couldn't tell ya. Dis information came from a couple new sources. Real fresh. Is there a Party Stone? I coulda sworn that's what someone told me. I could be wrong. I'll see what I can dig up."

"He's lying, Tivan," the Grandmaster said. He swiped the second Wishing Ore and stuffed it into his satchel. "I'm taking this in lieu of killing you, Pungo. Thanks again! Please extend my condolences to your wife. Being married to you is a real tragedy. Come, brother. I must speak with you outside." The Grandmaster exited Pungo's Pawnshop in a huff. The Collector followed behind.

Once outside, they heard Pungo wailing to himself from deep inside the building. His cries echoed across the alleyway.

"Oh, how the mighty have fallen," the Collector said, staring daggers at his brother.

"And to whom are *you* referring?" asked the Grandmaster.

The Collector smirked. "Pungo, of course."

The Grandmaster and the Collector had seen the universe take many shapes over their lifetimes.

Together and apart, they'd experienced things that defied comprehension. It was a strange thing to have in common. Neither had seen the other in person in a long while. The galaxy was large. Travel was expensive. As family members often do, they drifted apart. These weren't excuses, merely truths. Their lives had changed drastically since their last encounter. At this moment in time, neither was willing to share those details. They had to relearn how to trust each other first.

The Grandmaster winced as he looked the Collector up and down. "Who's dressing you these days? You look like you're being styled by a half-blind Zoobaazian," he scoffed.

"What an absolute pleasure it is to see you again, too, En Dwi," the Collector said in the driest of tones. "Your wit and charm are as sparkling as ever."

"I'm just having a bit of fun with you, brother. You remember *fun*, don't you? We used to have it before we became such manic adversaries, back when we were younglings," the Grandmaster said. "So are you going to show me around your disgusting toilet planetoid or not?"

"Forgive me for not rolling out a red carpet. I only give the star treatment when dealing with an actual *star*," the Collector said.

The Grandmaster spotted something in the distance and didn't acknowledge his brother's remark. Among the dark alleys of Knowhere, a glowing blue dot blinked above a thick dungeon door. On the outside, it didn't look like much; however, the Grandmaster knew that behind that door was an exclusive members-only lounge with no name. Some called it the Blue Dot, others just called it Blue. Most people didn't call it anything because they were unaware it existed. The door was guarded by an eight-foot-tall demon with muscles the size of melons, dressed in a three-piece suit.

"I see an old friend. Let's go get a drink," said the Grandmaster. He tossed his satchel at the Collector, who stumbled to catch it.

"No, no, no. I'm not going in that place," the Collector said. "I have things to do elsewhere."

"Are you worried you won't get in looking as foolish as you do? It'll be fine. I know the bouncer. Loosen up and come have a drink. It's a special occasion. *I'm* in town."

The Collector considered the offer and relented. "One drink," he said.

As they approached the establishment, the bouncer smiled to reveal a mouth full of wide, ivory fangs. "There he is! My man!" the bouncer exclaimed. "Looking good, Grandmaster."

"Kuda!" the Grandmaster cheered. "What a flatterer. I see you're still strong. Thick. Sturdy. If I recall correctly, your fighting skills are something to behold. And I *always* recall correctly. The last time I saw you, you were covered in blood and your enemy's entrails, screaming to the heavens in victory."

"Ah yes! My birthday party," Kuda recalled. "Those were good times."

"Need any side work?" asked the Grandmaster.

"I'm in need of a bodyguard. Help me out, and I'll make it worth your while."

"I wish I could, but I'm all booked up. Working this job and pursuing my art degree on the side," Kuda said. "Though, one of these days, I promise to come check out that Contest of Champions you've got going on Sakaar. Heard it's a scene."

The Grandmaster's grin melted. Once again, he was reminded of something he wished to forget. "Let's not discuss that now. We're here to relax and enjoy ourselves. This is my brother!" he said, pushing the Collector forward.

Kuda looked him up and down. "I don't know. He looks like he's been styled by a half-blind Zoobaazian. And he definitely can't bring that satchel in here without a search."

The Grandmaster put his arm around Kuda's bulky frame. "I agree with you wholeheartedly. This man is a pitiful person with no sense of style. But! He's also my brother. The satchel contains a Wishing Ore. My gift to him on, this, his birthday. I spent my last remaining funds to buy it. Isn't that nice? You don't want to turn this poor man away on his birthday, do you? Let him in. For *me*, Kuda."

Kuda's brow furrowed. "Both of you head to the back booth," the bouncer said, opening the door. "Joolz will fix you up. Everything is on the house."

"You spoil me, Kuda," the Grandmaster said. He took a thin business card from his robe and stuck it in Kuda's suit pocket. "Whenever you're ready to get back in the ring, you call me. Promise? I look forward to seeing what beautiful works your art degree yields." He and the Collector slipped into the building, down a long hallway. "Kuda is wonderful, isn't she?"

"That demon was female?" asked the Collector.

"You couldn't tell? And here I thought you knew a thing or two about a thing or two," the Grandmaster said. When they reached the end of the hallway, they pushed open another door together and were welcomed by a warm blue light. The intimate lounge bustled with activity. Gorgeous beings laughed, danced, and mingled, sipping drinks and enjoying one another's company. This was where they went when they didn't want to be bothered by the dregs of Knowhere, all the more treasured for its being a port amid the peasant storm of the rest of the planet. Soothing music filled the air. Luminescent beads dangled from the ceiling, pulsing to the steady beat.

The Grandmaster was pleased. "Let's unwind, shall we?"

CHAPTER 3

As the Collector moved through the lounge, past the casual revelers, he wondered if it was a mistake to be seen in public. Since *the incident* involving his museum, he'd become paranoid. He felt people staring at him, whispering. Maybe it was all in his mind. He wasn't quite sure anymore. He'd grown accustomed to the life of a hermit. Hiding out at home and sulking weren't ideal, but they had become comfortable. Out in the open, he felt exposed. His emotions were raw. He felt nervous. On top of all that, he hadn't prepared himself for what was about to happen. A one-on-one conversation with his brother was like a game, and the Collector wasn't interested in playing. But now he had no choice.

The Grandmaster did not appear to suffer from

any of his brother's insecurities. He glided through the room like a king, saying hello to old acquaintances as he passed, pausing briefly. He loved the attention. A few familiar faces were confused to see him on Knowhere, but he'd walk away before they had a chance to ask about it. His eyes moved across the crowd, calculating. He was always looking for someone he could use for his own purposes.

They arrived at the back of the lounge to find a large metal box rising from the floor. Inside was a roomy booth and a private bar. The VIP section. A short, stout, tentacled creature wearing a stark white frock appeared out of thin air to greet them. Each of his six feelers was shaking a myriad of colorful elixirs. "Hello, gentleman. My name is Joolz. I'll be your mixologist this fine evening," the creature said, whipping his tentacles in every direction. "How we feelin'?" The brothers stared at him in silence. "Alrighty, then, I've got a lot of great things for you to try tonight. I'd love to start you off with a Mumb Melon Spritzer or some Zaxus Blood. If you're ready to take this to the next level,

I'm also down to make a couple of flaming Surtur Shooters. What's your poison?"

"Make us whatever gaudy drinks you want, and then be quiet," groused the Collector. "We won't be here very long."

Joolz placed two empty glasses on the table and filled them with bubbling neon liquid. "Cheers. If you need me, just holler," he said, fading away.

The Grandmaster smiled at his brother. He retrieved the concoction, took a small sip, and leaned back in his seat. "Are you not speaking to me now?" he asked, swirling his drink. "You're so rude, Tivan. Lighten up. We're at a social establishment. A members-only club. Be grateful. I'm still waiting for my thank-you, by the way."

The Collector collected his drink and swigged. "Thank you," he said softly. He considered asking his brother about the *rumors*. The scraps of information their mutual associates had relayed to him. One such involved the Grandmaster's mocking the Collector upon hearing the news that he'd tragically lost his museum, saying that he'd known all along his brother would get what was coming to him. That information came from more than three sources. Were they trustworthy? Not entirely. Regardless, the Collector knew his brother to be jealous of his achievements. He saw it in his eyes. Now the Grandmaster was looking for weaknesses. The Collector wasn't about to let himself become a target.

"How long has it been since we've spent a length of time together?" the Grandmaster asked. "My memory is so hazy these days. There's a wonderful tea that helps with that. I'll have to find some while I'm here. Are there tea shops on Knowhere? There have to be, right? Don't worry, I'll find them. You know, I've actually been thinking about you a lot lately. To be honest, I had a feeling we'd run into each other. It's all very cosmic. Do you ever get those kinds of feelings? Maybe it's just because of who we are and the things we've seen, but sometimes I get the impression that we're connected to the universe in a deeper way than most. Isn't that something?"

The Collector sighed loudly, downing his drink in three quick gulps.

"I know you have questions, Tivan. I do, too. Why don't you ask me what you want to ask me instead of sitting there like a shivering coward?"

The words stung the Collector, so he stung back. "Right, then. What are the personal failures that brought you here? What recent pain have you endured? What has chewed you up and spat you out in your brother's backyard? Clearly, we've both suffered losses; otherwise, we wouldn't be dealing with Pungo. Tell me what happened on Sakaar, tell me what you want from me, and then leave my domain. In that order."

The Grandmaster was impressed. "My brother's spine has appeared!" he exclaimed. "This is the Taneleer Tivan I like to see. But, let's be honest, your *domain*? That's a bit dramatic. You're too good for this scrap heap. Really. We both are. This whole planetoid is a dump. Knowhere is best left to Ravagers and all the other scum-sucking space cretins."

"Answer the question."

Despite his posturing, the Grandmaster had become uneasy. He hadn't actually expected his brother to be so direct. "Joolz!" the Grandmaster shouted. The tentacled mixologist materialized in an instant. "Could we get some hors d'oeuvres? A tray or two of snacks? Nothing cheap. I want rare meats topped with exotic flowers. Decadent flavor combinations. You understand?"

Joolz nodded. "I'll see what I can do."

"Oh, and you're not listening to our conversation from whatever spirit world you're disappearing into, are you?" the Grandmaster asked.

"No, sir," replied Joolz. "I don't disappear into a spirit world. I disappear into the kitchen, which is over there." He pointed to a small metal doorway a few feet away.

"Good. Good. Now, be gone," the Grandmaster said as Joolz faded away.

The Collector remained silent, glaring at his brother in anticipation.

The Grandmaster took another sip of his drink

and let out a long-suffering sigh. "All right, Tivan, I'll talk. Just stop *frowning* at me. It's grossly undignified. *Yes*, as you may have suspected, things on Sakaar didn't go the way I'd planned. After a series of unfortunate events, I decided to travel," the Grandmaster said. "Because of said events, I've made some persistent enemies. I'm unable to stay in one place for too long. Knowhere, despite its numerous, ugly flaws, suits my needs. It makes for the perfect hiding place."

"And what? You want *me* to house you?" the Collector asked.

"Ha! No," said the Grandmaster. "Not unless you want to. Much of my wealth has been frozen for reasons I can't get into at the moment. Otherwise, I'd be in a luxury suite at some celestial villa. Trust."

"This is very interesting," said the Collector. "I never knew how much I would enjoy hearing you like this."

"I don't *need* your help. I never have. I merely thought it would be ideal for the two of us to end our estrangement and actually spend time together," the Grandmaster said.

"If you'd like me to house you, I'll need to hear the words," the Collector said, leaning in close. "Say them."

The Grandmaster took a deep breath. "May I stay with you, *brother*?" he asked.

The Collector weighed his options carefully. If he said yes, he'd be inviting his brother's constant ridicule, but if he said no, he'd be rejecting family. And family wasn't something he had in abundance. In the end, the Collector went with his instincts. "Yes," he replied. "You may stay with me for as long as our temperaments will allow."

The Grandmaster raised his glass high. "I can't wait to see the museum," he said, taking a drink. "I hear it's been through its fair share of changes as of late."

At the entrance to the lounge, a sudden commotion erupted. Boisterous Cackalorns pushed their way through the space, knocking over patrons and spilling drinks without a care. They spied an empty booth nearby and commandeered it.

Cackalorns weren't known for their manners, to say the least. They were crude country folk. Angry for the most part. Unwilling to abide by change in a galaxy where change was constant. Their loose skin was pale. Their droopy complexions marked by years of hard living. Big heads. Tiny bodies. Spiky scalps and gummy grins. They wore the flag of Cackalor proudly, wrapping it across themselves in a variety of combinations, telling anyone within earshot about their planet's numerous wars. Worst of all, they were always looking for a fight.

"Oi! Where's the dog with the tentacles?!" their leader screeched. "We need a round of Flazen Milk barrels! Right now!"

"Oi!" the other Cackalorns shouted in unison.

Their presence made the Grandmaster cringe. "How do people like that get in here?" he asked. "Private clubs weren't meant to accommodate trash, but I suppose money talks these days."

"Ha! Money talks every day," said the Collector. "Ignore them."

The rowdy Cackalorns slammed their fists onto their table in impatience, calling loudly for their drinks and stomping their feet, making the floor shake with a rippling effect that expanded up and through the lounge. The racket was driving the Grandmaster crazy. "This is ludicrous. I'm going to complain," he said, pushing away from the table.

"*Don't*. It will only make things worse," said the Collector. "We need not stay here any longer. Let's be gone and done with it."

"But we haven't even gotten our food yet!" the Grandmaster exclaimed. "I'm saying something." Before he had a chance to tell the Cackalorns to pipe down, a thundering brute came stomping across the lounge. His bulky pink body was thick and boxy with skin like fine sand. The expression on his face indicated that he hadn't had a very good day. The brute was headed straight for the Collector.

"You're sitting in Yaan's area," he bellowed.

"That's fine. We're leaving," the Collector said, scooting out of the booth.

The Grandmaster threw up his leg under the table to stop his brother's exit. "Not so fast." He turned his attention to the brute. "Are *you* Yaan?" he asked. "Because, if you are, you're one of the most magnificent specimens I've ever encountered. Your frame alone intrigues me. It's as if an enormous brick has come to life! I like it."

The brute was visibly disturbed by the odd compliment. "Yaan says again: You're sitting in Yaan's area. Leave now, and Yaan will let you keep your limbs."

"Speaking in third person. Very powerful," the Grandmaster said. He slowly rose to his feet to address the brute directly. "Listen, Yaan, I have a proposition. I want you to be my new bodyguard. A young man like you needs steady work, no? I like your shape, and I imagine you could crush anyone who gets in your way. Am I right?"

"Yes," Yaan murmured.

"I had a feeling I was. Let me pose another question—have you ever done combat in an ooze pit? It's humiliating, but it pays well." The Grandmaster sat back down, comfortable he now had Yaan under his spell, putting his legs up on the table and crossing them. "So it's settled. You'll be my new bodyguard. What a weight off my shoulders. It's been such a long search. I'm happy to finally put it behind me."

Yaan just stood there, growling.

"Yaan, I'm making you the offer of a lifetime here." The Grandmaster's voice took on an imploring tone, noting the deal wasn't quite as sealed as he'd thought. "I urge you to be quiet and take it. From one professional to another. Or, I promise, you'll end up very, *very* sorry. That I can promise you. Do you know who I am?"

"You are a wafer of a man that Yaan will break into pieces if you do not leave," Yaan growled.

The Collector smacked his brother's feet off the table. *"Get. Up,"* he spat through gritted teeth.

The Grandmaster ignored Tivan, looking directly at Yaan. "Make me," he said. Yaan grabbed him by his collar, lifted him from his perch, and tossed him onto the ground as if he were no heavier than a feather.

"Hand me a weapon, Tivan," the Grandmaster whispered.

"I don't *have* a weapon, En Dwi," the Collector replied under his breath.

Yaan glared at the Grandmaster. "Yaan recognizes you," he said. "You kidnapped Yaan's brother and made him battle monsters for sport."

"Oh!" exclaimed the Grandmaster, visibly pleased. "Was he any good?"

"He perished," Yaan snarled.

"Are you sure that was me?" asked the Grandmaster. "Because, I'll be honest, if he looked anything like you, I would have remembered."

Joolz, the mixologist, appeared carrying a tray of piping-hot hors d'oeuvres, small morsels of pink topped with brightly colored blossoms. "Who's ready for some tasty treats?" he asked. "Oh, hey, Yaan! How's tricks?"

Yaan yanked Joolz's tentacles with force, tied them into a knot, and swung the creature with such might that he landed on the table of the feisty Cackalorns. He then turned his attention to the Grandmaster. "Your turn," Yaan snarled, lifting his boot into the air. Before he could bring down his massive foot, a wild Cackalorn jumped on his back and began wailing on him with fury.

"Oi!" their leader shouted, ripping his shirt to shreds and wrapping it around his fists. "For the glory of Cackalor!" In an instant, the lounge descended into chaos.

"*That* escalated quickly," the Grandmaster gasped. He pointed toward the kitchen door. "*Now* we can go."

The Collector grabbed his brother's satchel, and they rushed through the bustling galley and out the back door, Cackalorn shouts trailing behind them.

"What an unexpected thrill!" the Grandmaster declared as they tumbled into the night. "But where is your spine, brother? You rolled over for that obnoxious flesh mound so *easily*."

"I didn't want any trouble."

"And yet it finds you anyway."

"He wanted his table!" the Collector exclaimed. "You should have let him have it instead of trying to recruit him for your absurd model search."

"*Bodyguard* search. And I can't believe what I'm hearing. Are you not the great and powerful Collector? Stand your ground, brother! Own your station!" The Grandmaster grinned. "Rooming together is going to be great fun, isn't it? Let's get going. I can't wait to see my new *home*."

CHAPTER 4

"What a dump!" the Grandmaster exclaimed as they entered the Collector's museum a little while later. "It looks so empty. Give me a tour."

"All in due time, brother. Slave!" the Collector bellowed.

Keelan bounded into the room like an eager Terran canine, thrilled to see her master. "Welcome home, merciful Collector," she beamed.

"We have a guest," the Collector announced. "My brother."

Keelan gasped, her breath escaping her momentarily. "*THE Grandmaster.* What a pleasure it will be to serve you. My master rarely speaks of you, but when he does—"

"Stop," the Collector said. "That's enough."

"May I take your bags, Grandmaster?" asked Keelan, switching tacks.

"He has no bags. Only this." The Collector held up the satchel and threw it at Keelan. "Be very careful, as that contains precious cargo. Prepare a cot in the basement."

"A cot?! In the basement?!" shrieked the Grandmaster. "No, no, no. That won't do. I require warm linens. High thread counts. Do you have a hot tub? Where will I soak my feet?!"

"I'm giving you all I have at the moment," the Collector replied. "Be thankful."

"I shall unfurl the guest cot, then assemble a tasty meal for the both of you!" Keelan said.

"Any word on the identity of our thief?" asked the Collector. "Pungo informed me he's expecting a Dotaki skull. Investigate the matter immediately."

"Of course, great Collector. I haven't had much time to pursue any information, but—"

"I wanted this issue resolved as soon as possible," growled the Collector.

"It's only been a matter of hours since you gave

me the task. I've been busy doing so many other things, like…" She trailed off. "Well, I'm doing my best."

"Do better," the Collector threatened, waving her away to perform her duties.

"She seems nice," the Grandmaster commented after Keelan had left them. "Didn't ask about which foods I enjoy and how fluffy I like my pillows, but I'll chalk that up to nerves. Is someone stealing from you, Tivan? That's a serious matter."

"I'll not discuss this with you. Come," the Collector said, waving his brother into the museum's main area. The Grandmaster let his eyes wander across every inch of the menagerie, taking it all in. He prepared his game, the judgment radiating from his body. He wanted to figure out his brother's weaknesses and found them everywhere he looked. It was apparent that the museum had sustained a traumatic event, confirming the rumors that the Grandmaster had heard. The Grandmaster wondered how he might take advantage of it.

"Is this it?" the Grandmaster poked. "I was under the impression you'd cultivated an impressive spread. At least that's what I'd heard in certain circles. 'A remarkable collection of exotica and a zoo full of beasties,' they said. A mutual friend told me you had a Sovereign Birth Pod. Is there more somewhere else in the museum, or is this all of it?"

Now that they had returned to the Collector's home turf, he felt in control once again. He wasn't about to let his brother take away the power he felt over his own domain. He chose his words carefully and delivered them in a patient tone. "There was an unfortunate *incident*. Items were lost. Things changed. I, however, endure," he said firmly. "Now. Let me fix you a refreshment." They ambled over to the study, where the Collector prepared his brother a tall glass of herbal elixir. "Have you ever tried that fruity concoction the Nova Corps serves at their formal events?"

"I don't get along with the Nova Corps," the Grandmaster replied.

"Neither do I, but I've employed a few under the table. It allows me to operate freely. They leave me to my work," the Collector said. He handed his brother the drink. "I imagine you'll quite like its tart flavor. Enjoy."

"*Mmmmmmm.* I can taste the herbs," the Grandmaster said, pursing his lips. He spotted his brother's chair. "What is this monstrosity?!"

"Get away!" the Collector exclaimed, pushing his brother away and taking a seat. "You go over there."

The Grandmaster collapsed onto a long sofa covered in soft pillows. "Now, *this* feels *good*," he said, extending his arms for a stretch. "Maybe I'll just sleep here."

"So tell me, what's truly brought you to my doorstep in such a state, brother?" the Collector asked. He sipped his drink in anticipation. "It must be more than just an ungrateful population. Start at the beginning. Don't leave anything out."

The Grandmaster lay back, stared at the ceiling,

and sighed. He appeared relaxed. His expression became wistful as he recalled recent events. "Have you ever *been* to Sakaar?" he asked. "It's filled with violence and chaos. Open wormholes littering the sky, spitting out debris from across the galaxy. Scavengers, vicious thugs, rummaging through it, all looking for the one thing that might be their ticket off the planet. News flash—there are no tickets off Sakaar. But I arrived there and saw potential. I used people's anger and frustration to make money. *A lot* of money. I arranged the Contest of Champions. A legendary gladiatorial tournament featuring the most powerful beings in the universe. The best of the best. Action! Drama! Spectacle! Each battle filled me with more satisfaction than I'd ever experienced in my life." The Grandmaster put his hand on his chest, closed his eyes, and smiled as if he were dreaming. "Such richness of species, each one struggling, tearing at one another for glory and sport. It was a beautiful thing to behold."

"How did you find these challengers?" the Collector inquired.

"Well, some of them I kidnapped. Some of them I stole. Some of them had nothing. So I gave them something, and they became mine. Like Scrapper 142. Oh, she was a good one. Tough gal. A warrior in face paint. You know how I adore face paint. Beautiful but threatening. I tried to get her to ride a winged horse just for fun, but I couldn't find one. Truth be told, she wasn't *mine* per se. Our relationship was transactional. She found me fighters, and I paid her for them."

"Was this venture of yours profitable?" asked the Collector.

The Grandmaster shot up like a bolt. "Oh, indeed it was," he said, preening. "People attended in droves. The crowds loved it. They'd tailgate all day, then pour into the arena like vermin. Seeing as I'm a consummate businessman, I exploited them to the hilt. Merchandising is where the real money is made, everyone knows that. Branded product! Fans buy it without thinking. Give them a little pomp and circumstance, and you'll get whatever is in their pockets. I had this device—the Cerebral Holographic Environment Nexus—that I used to project an enormous hologram of myself across the sky. The little bootlickers ate it up! I might as well have been their god."

The Collector was intrigued, to say the least, and more than a little envious. Not that he'd ever allow the Grandmaster to see that. "Did you have a favorite brawler?" he asked.

A warm look fell upon the Grandmaster's face. "My sweet *Champion*. My sweet, sweet *Champion*. Oh, I miss him so much. Truly. Madly. Deeply," he said, pausing for a moment of silence. "Thinking about him brings up many feelings."

"And you put all your faith in this Champion?"

"Not *all* my faith. *Most* of it. Believe me, I had other strong fighters. Loads of them. Korg, the Kronan rock man, for instance, was a solid specimen. Strong with a delicate and playful side. Always intriguing in battle. But then he went and betrayed me, the rocky ingrate. Started an entire revolution right under my nose. One day I'll find him and smash him to pieces for it. Then I'll take those pieces and scatter them throughout the galaxy just in case he tries to re-form himself. I don't know if he can do that, but I'd like to be prepared. Oh! You know who else was fun? Sparkles, the Lord of Thunder! You know him, yes? Blond. Infuriatingly handsome. Lost him in the uprising. Gone in the blink of an eye."

"Thor?!"

"I am a little bit, yes. He had a lot of potential."

"No. Not *sore*. *Thor*," the Collector pressed. "The Lord of Thunder you speak of is named *Thor*."

"Oh. I see. Here I thought you'd suddenly developed a speech impediment," the Grandmaster said. "I never cared about his name. Who *cares* about a prisoner-with-a-job's name?! That's just bad management." The Grandmaster suddenly remembered something. "He had a hammer at one time! I just now recalled one of my underlings had mentioned it to me at one point. He didn't have the thing when he was spat out on my doorstep, but you should look into it. An item like that may interest you since you're so obsessed with preserving things," the Grandmaster said, taking a gulp of elixir.

"I *have* done business with Asgardians, you know."

"Ooh! What are *Asgardians*?" The Grandmaster perked up. "They sound lively. Can they fight?"

"Asgardians are citizens of Asgard, which is one of the Nine Realms. How are you unaware of this?" the Collector asked, incredulous at his brother's ignorance.

"Eh." The Grandmaster frowned. "Too much drama. I prefer to stay out of realm-y things, but I'd be delighted to hear your take on them."

"Well, Thor is a reckless, temperamental manchild. Lots of brawn and little brains, trapped in the body of a god. We've never crossed paths, but I've heard stories. Thor's a handful," the Collector explained. "But then again, so is his father, Odin."

The Grandmaster tilted his head thoughtfully.

"The Lord of Thunder has grown up quite a bit from what I gather. Which isn't saying much. I suppose he's had to. Adapt or die! Those are the rules of the universe. You should probably really try to get your hands on that hammer of his. It seems like something you'd want to display in your sad, little showroom."

The Grandmaster's ignorance frustrated the Collector. "Mjolnir isn't just some hammer. It's enchanted. I wouldn't even be able to lift it. You don't know what you're talking about."

"Enlighten me." The Grandmaster smirked.

I will do just that, you leering brat, the Collector thought.

"The name Mjolnir translates to 'that which smashes.' It was crafted by Odin from a piece of Uru, an indestructible Asgardian metal. It can withstand virtually anything. That's owed to the many enchantments that have been placed on the thing. That's how Thor controls the weather, among other elements. He and Mjolnir are forever linked as per the inscription: 'Whosoever holds this hammer, if he be worthy, shall possess the power of Thor.' Without it, he's just a lost boy."

"Interesting," the Grandmaster said, stroking his chin. "His lack of hammer didn't stop him from ruining my life."

"Oh?" the Collector asked without any sympathy. "How grave."

The Grandmaster shifted uncomfortably in his seat. He wanted to tell his brother the truth and be done with it, but now was not the time. Not yet. "I've got a question for you," he said, shifting the conversation. "What if someone else *becomes* Thor? Would that person inherit the power? Would they be able to wield the hammer? Is something like that even possible?"

"I suppose if the mantle of Thor were to be bestowed upon, say, a frog, then it would make sense that the frog would inherit the abilities as well."

The Grandmaster considered the possibilities.

"I'd rather see it in the hands of a Korbinite. Not just any old Korbinite, though. He'd have to be exceptional. That makes the task of finding one even harder, since they're a boring, tedious people. With some cybernetic enhancements and experimentation, a Korbinite with an Asgardian hammer could pose a formidable threat. I'm titillated just thinking about it!"

Watching his brother's delight made the Collector miss gossiping with him the way they used to do when they were younger. Back when the stakes were low and they understood each other like no one else.

"You know who rubs me the wrong way?" the Grandmaster asked. "The Lord of Thunder's brother. *Loki.* He's a slimy little trickster, isn't he? One minute he's on your side, and the next he's declaring war on you. The grinning swindler."

"I did business once with Lady Sif and Volstagg. They're Asgardian warriors," said the Collector. "They seemed reasonable. I even bowed to them so they'd feel like they were in control of the situation. Treat an Asgardian like royalty, and they'll give you anything you want."

"Good to know. And what did these Azburgians have that interested you?" the Grandmaster asked.

"*Asgardians.* They presented me with an item known as the Aether," the Collector said stiffly, leaning back in his chair.

"What is it? Where do you keep it? Will you tell me?" the Grandmaster asked.

The Collector glared at his brother. "No," he said dismissively.

"Of course, you won't. But that's fine. I'll find out somehow," said the Grandmaster. "Though if I were you, I'd put it on display for all to see. Show my enemies what power really looked like. Assuming this Aether has some degree of cosmic relevance. Knowing *you,* it might be some simple, nostalgic item from your youth. A lost trinket whose only value resides in your memory."

"Need I remind you, you are not me," said the Collector. "*And* you have no idea of the Aether's origins or abilities. *I suggest you move on from this line of questioning.*" In his museum, the Collector controlled the conversation, and now was not the time to discuss the Reality Stone nor any of the other Infinity Stones. He tried to steer the Grandmaster in a different direction. "I'd rather you regale me with more of these amazing gladiatorial matches of yours. I'm positively riveted by your tales," he said. "Tell me more about this Champion. He sounds incredible." The Collector noticed his brother's glass was empty. He rushed to fill it with more elixir. "What was his name?"

"The Hulk." The Grandmaster's voice was filled with longing. "Do you know of him?"

Of course the Collector knew of the Hulk. The name alone made him tingle. The Hulk was exactly the type of beast he dreamed of showcasing in the museum, though he didn't have the proper facility to contain a creature of such stature. The Hulk's value was immeasurable despite the safety risk he posed. There had been rumors he'd been floating through the cosmos, so it was no surprise he ended up on Sakaar. The Collector was only mildly jealous his brother had the chance to experience the Hulk's ferocity in person. He decided to be cheeky nonetheless. "The Hulk is from Ergonar, I believe? An orange fellow with a ponytail, if I'm not mistaken."

The Grandmaster shot the Collector a scornful look. "No, no, no! He's from Earth! And he's magnificent. A mammoth being. Muscles the size of meteors. Green skin. A wonder to behold. My showstopper. My *Champion*! A bulging monster who, as I found out later, is actually a ticking time bomb called Bruce Banks."

The Collector couldn't pass up the chance to correct his brother. *"Banner,"* he shot back. "The Hulk's name is *Bruce Banner*."

The Grandmaster raised an eyebrow. "So you *do* know him? You little deceiver."

"No, I don't. All I know is the Hulk is actually a brilliant human scientist when he's not a rampaging rage monster. This was told to me by several contacts. Assuming they're trustworthy, he sounds like a truly fascinating specimen."

"He'd make an excellent addition to your collection. *If* you could contain him. Not that you could," the Grandmaster said. He craned his head around in a dramatic act of surveillance. "From the looks of it, you're in need of an attraction or two. This place has really thinned out."

"Things are picking up. Everything is cyclical."

"Indeed," the Grandmaster said. He took a swig and sighed. "I miss it so much. Sakaar. The Contest. I forgot to tell you that whoever defeated the Champion would get to ask me for a gift. Whatever they wanted. No strings. And I would give it to them. Isn't that nice? It always made me feel better. I needed something to balance out all the people I've melted out of spite. And there have been many. I really do love a public execution. Oh well. No one's perfect." The Grandmaster raised his glass. "Onward and upward."

Just then something shattered in the kitchen....

Keelan rushed into the room. Her hands waved back and forth frantically as she gasped for air.

"What is happening, slave?!" the Collector demanded.

Keelan inhaled sharply. "I was beginning to prepare a delicious meal for both you and the Grandmaster when I remembered I'd missed a spot of dust earlier during my cleaning. Then *that* made me remember that I hadn't finished taking the second inventory of the day like you'd asked. Seeing as I do not like to disappoint you, I felt it was important to complete all my given tasks before embarking on a new one."

Keelan's long-winded reply grated on the Collector's nerves. "Get to the point. What was that sound? What have you wantonly destroyed this time?"

"Do not worry, great Collector. Your menagerie is just fine. I merely dropped a plate of appetizers. Something to tide the both of you over as you caught up. I shall go pick them up now. Since they're not suitable for consumption, shall I feed them to the Xandarian Boulder-Crusher in the basement? That way they will not go to waste."

The Collector was over it. "Yes. Fine. Do that. Leave us."

Keelan zipped away, but not before winking at the Grandmaster while the Collector was distracted.

"What a little enigma Keelan is," remarked the Grandmaster. "I like the blue scales. She's very lean. Can she arm wrestle?"

"No."

"You've got a Xandarian Boulder-Crusher in the basement?!" asked the Grandmaster. "Where I'm supposed to sleep?"

"He's locked in a cage. You'll barely notice," replied the Collector. "Finish your story. What happened on Sakaar?"

Grandmaster released a long, tired exhale. "The Lord of Thunder, Korg, and all their nasty little friends staged a revolt. People don't like battling to the death, apparently. But, in the end, we decided to call it a tie and move on."

"Revolts do not end in ties," the Collector said with marked suspicion.

The Grandmaster simply smirked. "You got me," he admitted. "The truth is...*I won*. But everyone was so seethingly *jealous*. I just had to get out of there. Can't be around all that negative energy."

The Collector remained skeptical.

"Oh, you just have to know *everything*, don't you?" the Grandmaster scoffed. "They pillaged my beautiful tower, all right?! All the miserable species I bestowed purpose on ended up betraying me. My Champion left. There was a lot of destruction and a little bit of terror. I did some things I'm not proud of and lost some prized vintage spaceships along the way. The bottom line is that I am currently without resources. Thinking about it is so depressing. Obviously, I was no longer on good terms with the citizens of Sakaar, so a new journey was in order. I came here because..." His voice trailed off. He finished his drink and noticed a trace of red sand at the bottom of his glass. Understanding mixed with a bit of admiration flashed across his face. "Well played, brother. I'd know the sight of Kvellian Truth Paste anywhere. I wondered why I felt so tingly and truthful. But, ugh, what a rancid taste."

The Collector maintained his poker face. "I don't know *what* you're talking about."

"Well, you got the information you wanted. My pretenses have been shed. Now it's time for you to shed yours." The Grandmaster's face brightened menacingly. "You think I didn't know what the Aether is, brother? As a youngling, you used to mumble about it in your sleep. *Every. Single. Night.* Quit dawdling and get real. *Show me your Infinity Stone.*"

CHAPTER 5

The Grandmaster stared unblinkingly at his brother. "I can tell I touched a nerve," he said, grinning from ear to ear. "So where is it? Or *them*. Though, if what I know of the Infinity Stones is true, keeping them in close proximity to one another could be troublesome. You probably know that already. What with your lifelong obsession with them and all that."

The Collector remained silent as he sank farther into his chair, his hands gripping the sides.

"Are you afraid that by merely saying the words *Infinity Stones* out loud you'll somehow conjure dark forces? Ha! Who could imagine you'd be so afraid?"

"I fear nothing!" barked the Collector.

The Grandmaster launched himself up from his

perch. He put his hands on his hips, stared at his brother, and waited for a response. "Dark Elves are notorious tattletales. Don't you want to know what they told me?"

"I do not," said the Collector, jolting up from his seat. He did, but he'd never admit it—he didn't want to discuss the Infinity Stones. At least not yet. He still had to figure out if his brother was up to something, some sort of ulterior motive that had brought him to the Collector, before he divulged any secrets. "Are you ready to tour my menagerie now, En Dwi?"

"I suppose so," the Grandmaster huffed. "But would you mind addressing me as Grandmaster? I prefer it."

Of course you prefer it, the Collector thought. *You're a pompous egomaniac.*

"Anything for you, dearest brother. You are both *grand* and a *master*."

The Collector invited the Grandmaster into the central part of the museum, and they began their stroll. As they passed through the menagerie, waves of memories flooded the Collector's brain.

He pointed to the corner of the museum. "That's where I kept the Sovereign Birth Pod. I'd bought it from one of Ayesha's disgruntled underlings. He'd stolen it right out from under her. Paid for his crime with his life, so I've been told. The poor gentleman. I believe the pod was destroyed during the mishap, but I'm sure Ayesha has already got herself a brand-new one, ready to birth some strange thing."

He pointed toward an empty cage. "My Dark Elf escaped without a trace. As a prisoner, he was mouthy. A *tattletale*, as you said. I can only imagine how intolerable he must be in battle. As far as endangered species go, he was a find. There's a small part of me that misses his nightly screams. I hope he doesn't return to take his revenge."

The Collector moved to another large, empty case, its glass shattered and jagged. "Comparatively speaking, my Frost Giant barely said a word. He was cold, no pun intended. He and the Dark Elf used to motion to each other. I think they were trying to use some kind of dark magic to escape. One never knows with these creatures from other realms. I'm also reminded of the Xeronian female who lost her life during the chaos. She was docile, quiet. Never put up a fight after her initial kidnapping. It's a shame she passed, but the poor girl was simply in the wrong place at the wrong time. She was always well fed, so that's something. Carina used to read to her. It was sweet."

"Carina? Who's that?" asked the Grandmaster.

"It doesn't matter." The Collector noticed the Grandmaster watching him on the sly as they ambled through each barren exhibit. A glint of pity was in his gaze.

"I can see how much you treasured your collection," the Grandmaster offered, reaching for an item with a long handle and stiff bristles sitting alone on a shelf.

"That's an ancient Kree toothbrush," noted the Collector. "It's never been used."

"I'm not surprised. Kree aren't known for their dental hygiene."

"My collection of creature carcasses was mostly blown to bits. Some were easily replaceable, others were not," the Collector said, gesturing to a full moose skeleton. "That was a Terran beast, so I've been told. I've been reading about their history. It's very boring."

The Grandmaster pawed at an empty display. "What did this contain?"

The Collector's eyes lit up as he recalled one of his sentimental favorites. "An Earth space suit. One of the very first, if I'm not mistaken. I could be mistaken. So much of my Earth knowledge comes from unreliable sources. The suit was primitive. Orange and puffy, with a cumbersome helmet. Earth people are so precious when it comes to space exploration. If only they knew how much they had to learn. Let's move along."

They entered a separate wing of the museum, where the Collector had been keeping an assortment of his newest finds. They weren't as impressive as the prior assortment he'd lost in the incident, but they were notable enough. Something to help get him back on his feet, or so he thought. He spied a personal favorite. "The Celestial Javelin, said to have been tossed down from the sky by the eternal creators. That is, if you believe such nonsense," he said, taking the long weapon from its perch. "I got it at a discount. The workmanship is superb."

The Grandmaster swiped the spear from his grasp and pressed his fingers into it. "It's clearly made of synthetic materials," he said. "It's not real. You should be embarrassed having this here."

The Collector swiped it right back and returned the item to its place. "I'll sell it to a fool, then."

They strolled past new additions—a stolen Nova Corps helmet, the Mask of Secrets, and a stuffed avian creature of unidentifiable origin. The Collector whipped a small box off a nearby shelf. It was covered in peeling red felt. He opened the box to reveal a dull silver blade made of steel. "This is a Vandarian butter knife."

The Grandmaster was unimpressed. "Well, at least you have a Chitauri blaster," he said, looking at a weapon hanging from the ceiling.

"That's broken, and the Chitauri handyman who lives in the area has yet to return my calls," said the Collector. He noticed his brother was becoming bored. "Can I show you my canister of slugs? They emit a strange and pleasant sound when you pet them. Or maybe you'd like to see the Pandorian crystal necklace I was gifted by a very wealthy diplomat. It's nice. Expensive. You don't want to know what I had to do to secure it."

"I was under the impression you used to have a lot more *beings*," the Grandmaster remarked. "Do creatures and beasts no longer hold your interest?"

"How dare you ask me such an inane question?!" the Collector snapped. "Organisms are my passion. Had I the resources, I'd collect specimens from *every* planet in *every* star system, but, in case you hadn't noticed, I've had a rough go of it lately."

"I can see that," the Grandmaster softly replied.

"Can you *see*? *Can you really*?" The Collector boiled over with renewed anger. "You look at my museum, and you see *junk*. You see *trash*. But you don't know what I've *been through*."

"Then enough talking around it, brother. Cut the lard! Spill it, Tivan. What the devil happened to this place? Come out with it already. I know it must have something to do with one of those blasted Infinity Stones you've always been so pre-occupied with. Stop being so tedious!"

The Collector sighed. The Grandmaster was right—it was time to reveal the whole truth. The Collector couldn't stall his brother any longer. He beckoned him back through the museum to the lounge area and prepared a new round of drinks. This time, the Grandmaster made sure his didn't contain any curious substances.

"I remember it as if it happened yesterday. Trite but true," the Collector began. "My slave girl Carina destroyed my museum. She'd made an appointment for me with the Guardians of the Galaxy. At the time, they were a group of noth-ings. Still are. But this is not their story. It's mine. They arrived at my doorstep with something I'd wanted for quite some time: an Orb containing one of the Infinity Stones. The Power Stone, to be exact. As our negotiation progressed, I noticed Carina was uneasy. In an instant, she grabbed the glowing ingot, hoping it would somehow give her the power to destroy me. *Her master.* The one who clothed her and fed her. Can you imagine? She had the nerve to be unhappy with her treatment at my hands. She sought to free herself from luxurious captivity. Instead, the Power Stone exploded in her grasp, and she was incinerated, as was much of my museum. I was spared, along with a handful of items. The Power Stone was almost in my hands. I could taste its essence. It was so *close*… and then it was all over.…" He trailed off. "Since then, I've felt a myriad of emotions. Emptiness. Malaise. I've felt unfulfilled. Searching but never finding. My restlessness has driven me to the point of exhaustion. Piecing my menagerie back together has been challenging, but what else can I do? The Collector collects." He swiftly shook out of the moment. "Go ahead, brother. Make whatever snide comment you'd like. I can see one fighting to escape your thin lips."

"I don't need to mock your trauma," the Grandmaster said. His tone was even. His expression was borderline genuine. "Walking through your museum in its current state, I can see your suffering everywhere. It's wretched. But this is what happens when you play with forces beyond your control."

"And you would know about these forces? You know nothing! You don't understand what these Stones are truly capable of. You don't respect their power! You never have!"

"Then educate me!" the Grandmaster said. He lay down on the sofa and arranged his lithe limbs into a comfortable position. "I shall be your student."

The Collector was bemused, but he knew he had nothing to lose at this point. "Settle in, brother," he said. "And pay attention." He snapped his fingers, and the room dimmed. Brilliant bursts of light appeared in hologram form. The birth of the universe was happening in front of their eyes. The lesson had begun.

"The creation of the universe is so boring and predictable," the Grandmaster complained. "Get to the good part. Show me those gorgeous Stones."

With the flick of his wrist, the Collector activated a rainbow of vibrant colors that filled the room completely: red, blue, green, yellow, orange, purple. They swirled through the space like comets before forming themselves into the Infinity Stones. Each stone hung in the air, glowing like festive ornaments.

The Grandmaster was mesmerized by their beauty. "*This* is what I'm talking about," he breathed, his mouth agape. "They're extraordinary."

"They're more than that," said the Collector. "They are the sum of all things. The key to the universe. They're *everything*."

The Grandmaster wasn't so certain. "But *are they? Really?*" he asked. "The Stones are extremely impressive, but *everything*? I'm not convinced."

"Perhaps these images will change your mind." The Collector activated another hologram. This time behemoths stomped through the space, using the Infinity Stones' power to destroy everything in their path. "*Power* is everything, and the Infinity Stones have more power than your feeble mind could ever imagine. The gigantic entities you see before you are the Celestials. They're almighty beings that recognized that power and used the Stones to give themselves unimaginable gifts that allowed them to terrorize entire worlds. The Celestials worked in silence, wreaking havoc across any planet they desired. Eventually they lost control, and the Stones ended up in the hands of other, lesser species like the Kree, the Asgardians, and the Dark Elves. For centuries, the Stones changed these civilizations, some for better and others for worse. Only beings of immense strength could wield the Stones and use their abilities to the fullest extent. Lesser beings, such as humans, were unable to grasp their absolute power. Fascinating though they may be, when an inferior species makes direct contact with the Stones, they're ripped apart by the sheer force of the thing. It's a glorious and frightening sight. In order to protect these beings, the Stones were given defensive casings: the Orb for the Power Stone, the Scepter for the Mind Stone, the Tesseract for the Space Stone, the Eye of Agamotto for the Time Stone, and"—his voice hardened—"as you know, the Aether for the Reality Stone."

The five items containing the Stones materialized in front of the Grandmaster's eyes. "I'm quite taken by these," he said, surveying their regal forms. "What about that orange one? Where does that one live?"

"Nobody knows where or in what the Soul Stone resides," the Collector responded shortly. It was a sore point with him. "In any case, the casings make the Infinity Stones difficult to locate but not *impossible*. The Stones themselves are completely indestructible, you see. One could not crush them if they tried. Many have. The Stones are, without question, the greatest power in the universe. They even speak to one another. Isn't that curious?"

He glided through the glowing holograms. "The blue Space Stone allows cosmic travel. This is accomplished through teleportation and the opening of portals. Instant access to any location in the universe—provided the Stone is used correctly. If it's used unwisely, the results can be calamitous. The Space Stone is also an immensely powerful source of energy, currently in the Tesseract, a cubic containment vessel that ended up in the hands of humans but now is back in Asgard."

The Collector walked over to the sparkling yellow Stone and gave the hologram a gentle spin. "The yellow Mind Stone gives its wielder control over weaker minds and the ability to bend them to their will. Think of it: an army of slaves at one's beck and call."

The Collector paused to take a breath. This was the most difficult Stone for him to talk about. "The purple Power Stone, when pushed to its limit, can annihilate entire planets. The Stone was placed in the Orb, as a means of controlling its raw and dangerous energy. Fate only knows how long that will last. As one who was witness to just a fraction of a fraction of its abilities firsthand, I can say with certainty that the force within the Stone cannot be contained for long." The Collector let out an involuntary shudder and continued. "The wielder of the green Time Stone can travel through the ages and control the flow of time, on both a small and massive scale. They can change history to suit their needs, age an adversary into dust, or simply peek into the past or present. The Stone is also capable of creating a Time Loop that traps a being in the same moment for all eternity. I find that feature to be particularly wicked."

"And the orange one?" the Grandmaster asked. "What does it do?"

The Collector shook his head. "Just like we don't know where the Soul Stone is, we also do not know the extent of its full powers. It's the most mysterious of the Stones." The Collector narrowed his eyes at the Grandmaster. "The red

Reality Stone is an unpredictable and deadly force that allows its wielder to alter our very existence. Its shapeless form is known as the Aether, a fluid crimson mass that can possess a host body and give them unlimited strength and unpredictable power."

The Grandmaster snickered. "I didn't know all *that*," he said. "I would've thought that possession was a little too ghoulish for your taste. I'll need a demonstration. Let's see this Aether in action. We could do a test run on Keelan!"

"Cosmic death rocks aren't something I feel comfortable showing off at the moment," the Collector said.

"Oh really? I see," the Grandmaster said. A tinge of doubt was in his voice. He lifted himself from the sofa. "I think I'll have another glass of that delightful elixir now. Sans truth potion, of course."

"Sit down. I'm not finished yet," the Collector grumbled.

The holographic Stones chased one another

through the air, coming together to assemble the bright hologram of a golden glove. Its glow illuminated the room. "While each Infinity Stone possesses a singular ability, they can also be used in unison. The *Infinity Gauntlet* channels the power of all the Stones at the same time. This is no easy task. All those who have attempted it have perished. The gauntlet connects directly to its bearer's mind. It can be overwhelming to an *inexperienced* being. It's unclear who built it, though I have my suspicions."

The Grandmaster watched his brother as he gazed reverently at the Infinity Gauntlet's brilliance. "My, my, my. You're positively enthralled. All this time, I never understood the depth of your obsession. These Stones have comforted you in your time of need, haven't they? This quest has kept you occupied for quite a while, made you feel not quite so alone, hasn't it, Tivan?"

The question aggravated the Collector. He fought to keep his composure, not wanting his brother to see him lose control. What soothed him were memories. His vibrant recollections of the Infinity Stones. As a youngling, before he knew of their existence, he dreamed of them, swirling in the sky at night, their glow forever imprinted in his mind. They were colorful and mysterious. Power beyond his wildest imagination. He'd wake in the morning and scribble their shapes from memory. When he grew older and discovered the nature of things, he made it his quest to acquire them. He traveled the cosmos and scoured the galaxy, engaging with the best and worst of the universe, yet the Stones evaded his grasp. Despite that fact, his desire never waned—if anything, their elusiveness only further intensified his need to possess them. The Infinity Stones made the Collector who he eventually became. Their histories were tied to one another for eternity. "Yes," he said. "This quest has kept me occupied for as long as I can remember. He who controls the Infinity Stones controls everything."

"All right then, brother, let us find them," the Grandmaster said. *"Together."*

CHAPTER 6

"Dinner is served!" Keelan said, grinning ear to ear. She placed a tray of grotesque fish heads on a table in the study. They were charred to a crisp and covered in crumbled leaves. "My mother used to make them on Zoobaaz. I hope I followed her recipe correctly. She used to tell me they'd bring my belly good luck."

The Grandmaster cringed at the stench from the platter. "They're staring at me," he said, pushing the tray away. "And they smell like something that's been dredged out of a sewage system."

"Get these out of here!" the Collector scolded. "I told you never to make those monstrosities ever again. I detest them, and I detest hearing about your family!"

Keelan removed the tray, head down, and retreated to the kitchen.

"If you don't eat soon, you'll end up extremely disagreeable, Tivan," the Grandmaster snickered. "What's *her* story anyway? I assume it's tragic."

"She moved to Knowhere because of a dream. I couldn't tell you what it was about. I believe she wanted to *help people*? I can't recall. After Carina's betrayal, I was hesitant to even acquire another slave, but then I saw Keelan, begging on the street. Her dream had perished along with her source of income. She was in need of guidance, so I took her in and gave her purpose once more. She surrendered to me completely. In the beginning, I thought she might have been up to something, but that was just my paranoia speaking. You can't blame me, given the horrid betrayal I'd only recently suffered. The truth is, she's too dim to know any better. She couldn't deceive me if she tried. Without me, she'd be back on the streets, scrounging for scraps. That's not a life she wants. She knows her place, and, for that, I'm grateful."

"Aw, what a kind employer you are," the Grandmaster commented.

Keelan raced back into the room. "Collector, sir, I must leave the museum on an errand at once," she said, out of breath. "I do not wish to leave you without refreshment, but I've just received some important information."

The Collector's eyes lit up. "Concerning?"

Keelan didn't want to go through the details of the museum's recent theft with the Grandmaster listening in. She chose her words extra carefully. "I've inquired with an associate of mine regarding the matter we discussed earlier."

"Say no more!" the Collector exclaimed. "Do what you must to secure the information you require, then *come right back*."

The Grandmaster tapped Keelan on the arm as she began to exit. "I'm looking for a bodyguard. Interested?"

"Leave her be, En Dwi. Be gone, slave," the Collector said, waving Keelan away.

The Grandmaster bristled. "You must really

stop using the *s* word, Tivan. Get with the times," he said. "And if I were you, I wouldn't be so cavalier about her intentions. If there's anything I've learned, it's that people will turn on you like rabid animals. Be cautious."

The Collector took heed of his brother's warning. Was Keelan smarter than she seemed? He hadn't fully considered such a thing. Thinking about her immense absentmindedness, he wondered if it was simply a cover. A way to gain his favor. Was she a plant, carefully orchestrated by one of his numerous enemies, to destroy him from the inside? The prospect overwhelmed him.

The Grandmaster snapped his fingers in his brother's face. "Back to business, Tivan. These Stones. How do we know they aren't actually closer than they seem? For instance, what if the Eye of Agamotto is here on Knowhere? What if that's the Infinity Stone Pungo was referring to?" the Grandmaster asked, a gleam coming into his gaze. "An item that can bend time itself?! You'd be able to regain your former glory in the blink of an eye! You'd be able to right the wrongs of the past and correct the grave injustices you've suffered that have left your museum in shambles and your life such a mess."

"I'm not the *only* one whose life is a mess."

"You've got me there," said the Grandmaster. "Then we agree. Together, we'll track down this stray Stone, and all the other Stones thereafter."

"*We* do not agree," protested the Collector.

"Shall we shake down Pungo for more information? That's definitely a two-person job. He's like tub of living jelly," said the Grandmaster. "Speaking of, you're looking meatier these days. Depression snacking?"

The Collector sprung to his feet and rushed away in silence.

"I hope I didn't offend you!" the Grandmaster shouted after him. "You shouldn't be so sensitive. Yes, you're at a low point, and everyone knows it, but look on the bright side. As a betting man, I can assure you, the odds will shift in your favor one of these days. They have to. And if for some reason they don't, then consider that you were never meant for greatness."

A moment later, the Collector returned with a melon-size purple-hued crystal ball. He placed it on his workbench. "This is a crystalized cosmic embryo from a realm that replays Time Loops specifically centered on cross-dimensional forces from other quadrants of the universe."

"Handy."

"I believe I can use it to commune with other planes of existence and, in turn, find the current whereabouts of the Eye of Agamotto."

"Well, then, stop talking and fire it up!" the Grandmaster exclaimed, slapping his brother's back.

The Collector moved his hands across the round ball, caressing it with care. "I'm not exactly sure how to activate the thing," he conceded after a few moments of silence. "I bought it on a whim."

"Lonely nights at home watching the cosmic shopping channels? I've been in a similar place."

FZZZACK!

The lights went out in the museum. The Collector's hands vibrated as he gripped the pulsing embryo. His shocks of white hair stood on end. A deep purple hue papered over his eyes as he entered into a new state of awareness. "This is—this is…" the Collector stammered.

"Tivan? Don't toy with me. If you're possessed by some cosmic spirit, you have to tell me right now. Don't you dare use magic to hurt me. Don't you dare! And, for the record, it wasn't my intention to insult you before. I was having fun. Just want to be clear about that in case you were thinking of ending my life."

"SILENCE!" the Collector screamed. His voice echoed in the darkness as the museum shook with great force. A warm purple mist crept through the space, lingering near the ground. "The embryo is speaking to me. I will interpret the tale it seeks to tell." The mist began swirling itself into shapes, moving through the air like a million tiny serpents. It molded itself into the form of a human man. "This is *Stephen Strange*."

The Grandmaster huddled around the embryo. *"Go on."*

"Strange was a self-absorbed man. A doctor of medicine. His practice was everything to him. He became a perfectionist in both life and work. Then a tragic accident marred his hands. He was unable to deliver to the standards of perfection he demanded of himself. His frustration consumed him. Strange pushed away anyone who tried to help. The doctor wasn't used to being a patient. His ego prevented him from surrendering. He wished to control the process of healing as he did everything else in his life. But he couldn't. His physical body was in desperate need of repair and rehabilitation. His mental health suffered as well. Strange was a man without options."

The Grandmaster mockingly hoisted his finger in the air as if he'd just had a revelation. "And then he found some!" he exclaimed.

"Quiet," the Collector whispered. "Don't disturb this process." The purple mist formed itself

into a majestic mountain vista. "Without any available options, Strange went on a journey of self-discovery that took him to Kamar-Taj, a mountain temple in the country of Nepal. Tucked far away from the modern world and with good reason. Kamar-Taj was the home of The Ancient One, a tempered mystic who held the title of Sorcerer Supreme. She made sure the dark evil that threatened to destroy the universe was kept at bay with the help of her students, the Masters of the Mystic Arts. Though confused at first, Strange realized the key to healing would be studying under The Ancient One and her mages. They had the tools he needed to not just heal his hands but also heal his spirit. Sadly, he was rejected, but he remained a persistent force. Eventually, after some pestering, he was welcomed. He began his studies, but progress was hard won. The Ancient One was a gentle teacher at times and fierce when the situation required it, though she was not without secrets."

"Secrets," the Grandmaster purred. "Continue, please. Who else lives in this temple? I want to know about the rest of these *mages*."

"Mordo was The Ancient One's longtime associate. His job was to recruit and train the Masters of the Mystic Arts. As a dedicated servant of the light, he trusted The Ancient One without question and followed anywhere she led. Wong was the temple librarian. The keeper of the knowledge. Fiercely protective of his books and rightfully so. In the wrong hands, they were deadly weapons. Wong and Mordo helped Strange settle into his role as student. It wasn't an easy transition for any of them. Strange was fussy. His perfectionism was unshakable. As his studies progressed, he became extraordinarily anxious to master the power he felt was trapped inside himself. He'd read ledger upon ledger, but he still hadn't unlocked the magic he desperately sought. It made him *skeptical*."

"When does the Eye of Agamotto show up?" the Grandmaster muttered, growing impatient.

The pulsing purple mist crept across his body, slowly coiling around him like a serpent.

"The embryo would like you to remain silent," the Collector instructed.

"I can do that."

"Before arriving at Kamar-Taj, Strange believed he knew everything there was to know about existence. Then The Ancient One revealed to him the vast Multiverse, an infinite number of worlds without end. Some filled with light and hope. Others consumed with darkness and hate. Forces from beyond would consume *everything* if given the opportunity. Strange was shocked, to say the least. The Masters of the Mystic Arts guarded Earth against this darkness. They learned their trade by studying ancient practices that allowed them to harness universal energies. They drew power from other dimensions and used it to cast spells and conjure weapons. They learned to shape reality with their thoughts. They were magicians and sorcerers of the highest order. To fight the dark, the masters built a series of Sanctums around the globe that served as barriers between worlds."

The Collector removed his hands from the embryo. His purple eyes disappeared. The surrounding mist evaporated. The trance was cut short. He'd suddenly remembered something and scrambled over to a nearby bookshelf. After a bit of rummaging, he retrieved a small velveteen box, its color a deep green, dust coating it on all sides. He gently cleaned it off and took it to his brother.

"What is this?! What are you doing?!" the Grandmaster asked. "I want to know what happened!" His eyes widened as the Collector slowly opened the box. Inside was a bizarre metal ring: one long bar covering two knuckles.

"The Masters of the Mystic Arts used a handful of magical objects, but one more than any others," the Collector explained. "The sling ring enables its wearer to open fiery portals to other dimensions. It also allows them to travel long distances, blazing through the Multiverse in a matter of moments."

The Grandmaster was taken with the artifact.

"How does one wield it?" he murmured.

"The wearer puts it on their left hand and focuses on a destination while their right hand traces a circular portal in the air."

"That seems easy," the Grandmaster said. He slipped the ring onto his fingers, made a fist with his left hand, and waved his right pointer finger in a zigzag motion. Nothing happened. He tried it again. Same result.

The Collector watched his brother attempt the maneuver three more times before no longer being able to prevent a small chuckle from escaping him. "It's not real; it's a replica. I bought it at a discount from some old wizard. At least he told me he was a wizard," said the Collector. "Watching your expression shift from joy to disappointment gave me a small measure of fulfillment, En Dwi. Thank you for that."

The Grandmaster was miffed. "What a trick," he said, tossing the ring back into its box. "You just wanted to see me look foolish."

"Pipe down. You weren't even using it correctly,"

the Collector said, waving dismissively. He placed his hands on the embryo once again, but nothing happened.

"You've broken your cosmic egg!" exclaimed the Grandmaster. "It must've sensed your lack of true prowess and locked you out."

The Collector moved his hands all over the embryo to no avail. Its power had completely drained. "This is puzzling," mused the Collector.

"Back!" a voice called out from inside the embryo. The spectral mists returned with a vengeance. A gust of air pushed the brothers away from the embryo with force.

"What did you do, Tivan?!" the Grandmaster asked.

FZZZACK!

A small, glowing creature emerged from the embryo in a burst of purple light. Its eyes were wide and curious. It took tentative steps toward the Collector, seemingly unsure of its purpose.

The Grandmaster whispered into his brother's

ear. "I think your egg just hatched, Tivan."

The Collector stared down the brilliant hatchling. *"We were in the middle of something, if you don't mind,"* he growled. *"Either continue the tale we were engaged in or go back from whence you came. I won't be toyed with in this fashion."*

The hatchling stared at the Collector blankly. "I will continue the tale," it said meekly.

"Impressive show of power, brother," murmured the Grandmaster. "Keep it up."

"Where were we?" the hatchling said. It quickly recalibrated itself, channeling the cosmic energies from which it came to finish the story. "Ah yes. Let us continue. Once Strange was able to, at last, open his eyes in the truest sense, he embraced the world of magic and all its teachings. He learned of the Astral Dimension, a realm where the soul exists outside the physical body, and the Mirror Dimension, an unaffected place where a sorcerer can observe the natural world without interfering in it. Strange also increased his study of the temple's numerous texts. One in particular caught his interest. *The Book of Cagliostro* was a dark tome, filled with spells that often steered young pupils off the path of light. And there were pages missing. They'd been stolen by Kaecilius, a former Master of the Mystic Arts who formed a group of mystical zealots. Their mission was to unleash an evil entity from the Dark Dimension upon the earthly plane." The purple mist spread across the room, filling it completely. It cracked with thunder and lightning. A face emerged from the haze. It belonged to the dread god Dormammu. "Dormammu was more than just a demon. He was a cosmic force of nature with a fondness for mass destruction. Kaecilius and his zealots had made a deal. They would make it possible for Dormammu to enter the earthly place so that he would consume it."

"But why?" asked the Grandmaster. "Wouldn't this Kaecilius person lose everything when Dormammu arrived on Earth? Show me the logic."

"It's amusing that you seek to find reason in this madness," the Collector said.

The hatchling's eyes throbbed with purple energy. "To answer your question, Kaecilius had lost his everything when his wife passed away unexpectedly. He needed Dormammu to turn back time and resurrect her."

The Grandmaster rubbed his chin. "*Ahhh. Now* we're getting somewhere," he said. "The Eye of Agamotto should be making an appearance soon, and I am positively *tingling* over it."

"You needn't share such *personal* information," groused the Collector.

"Kaecilius believed time was limiting. Birth, death, the cycle of life. It was a slap in the face. In *his* estimation, humanity deserved to know what was *beyond* time. With Dormammu's help, they'd finally have a chance to escape it."

"By dying, I assume? That's a dim point of view. Or am I missing something?" the Grandmaster asked. The hatchling's eyes shot a beam of purple energy, burning a hole on the floor in front of the Grandmaster. "You know what? Keep going. I'll be quiet."

"The Time Stone," pressed the Collector. "Tell us of its role in all this."

The hatchling nodded obediently. "As Strange's studies progressed, he found himself entranced by the Eye of Agamotto, host of the Time Stone. The Eye could break apart the world and put it back together in new ways. Death and rebirth. He'd read about these abilities in *The Book of Cagliostro* and was instantly obsessed. One lone evening, Strange became compelled to test its power. He removed the relic from its perch, placed it around his neck, and concentrated. Suddenly, the Eye opened, glowing warm green. The Time Stone had awoken. Strange focused its energy on an apple from which he'd taken a bite, and in an instant, a new bite in the apple appeared. Then another and so on until all that remained of the apple was a rotted core. Strange had successfully accelerated time. The feeling fulfilled him, but he wasn't done with his experiment. He focused the Time Stone's power and returned the apple to its original state, thus completing the cycle. It was invigorating. Reality, perception, these things could be forever changed by the Eye of Agamotto. Strange wanted to know more; however, remember, *The Book of Cagliostro* was incomplete."

"Because Kaecilius stole some pages!" exclaimed the Grandmaster.

"Strange took matters into his own hands. He used the Eye of Agamotto to reverse time and return the missing pages, making the leap from novice to master. It was then that he finally understood the ominous threat he, and all of reality, faced. He'd seen the bigger picture and was ready to fully realize his true calling. But time was running out. A portal had opened above Hong Kong. Dormammu and the Dark Dimension were invading Earth. Worlds collided with fire and fury! Mass destruction unleashed upon an unsuspecting world! Kaecilius and his zealots were on a rampage. Wong and Mordo proudly stood on the front lines of battle, but, despite a valiant effort, they were unable to turn the tide. Wong lost his life. Darkness was on the cusp of reign until, at last, Doctor Strange arrived to stop it."

"Finally," the Grandmaster muttered with a roll of his eyes.

KRACKATHOOM! A whirlwind of purple mist surged through the museum.

"Strange used the Eye of Agamotto to turn back the clock. He stopped the destruction and saved countless lives. The city reconstructed. The devastation disappeared. Wong lived again. Time reset itself, but the battle wasn't over yet. The laws of nature continued to break as the Dark Dimension poked its tendrils into the earthly realm. Strange had one more mission to complete to save the planet from annihilation. He entered the void and came face-to-face with Dormammu himself. Strange was about to offer the dark god a bargain when Dormammu vaporized him into bits. Yet Strange reappeared. Dormammu stabbed him. Strange reappeared. The Doctor had learned how to adapt. He embraced the power of the Time Stone within the Eye of Agamotto and stuck Dormammu in a never-ending Time Loop. A single moment, on repeat, forever."

The Grandmaster gasped. "But that means Doctor Strange was stuck as well."

"Indeed. Doomed to suffer death at the hands of Dormammu over and over again. Strange had sacrificed himself, knowing that by replaying that moment, for all eternity, Earth would ultimately be spared. The loop was exhausting and painful for Strange to endure. He saw it as a small price to pay for protecting the planet he loved so much. A selfless act committed by a once-selfish man. Despite his very short time as a magic wielder, the Doctor was learning lessons. Meanwhile, Dormammu had caught on to Strange's plan. He was tired of being held prisoner in the Time Loop and begged to be set free. He was, at last, ready to bargain. Strange made his offer. He demanded that Dormammu remove his zealots from the earthly plane and never return."

"He made a deal with the devil?" asked the Grandmaster. "I see."

"Strange had no choice in the matter. It was the only way to win, and win he did. Dormammu yielded. The skies cleared yet again. Strange used the Time Stone to restore everything to its previous state."

"And to think, humans never even knew the lengths Strange and his companions went to to protect them. Thoughtless little things. Blissfully unaware of so much. It makes me wish I could rule them. Though they're too scrawny for my tastes. Except for my *Champion*, of course. He's an exception."

The Collector had remained silent, taking in the hatchling's tale, paying careful attention to each and every detail. At last, he'd learned the truth behind the Time Stone and was appeased. "That will be all, hatchling. Return to your crystal," the Collector decreed. "I may have need of you in the future, but, for now, I've heard enough."

The hatchling raised its arms, collecting the surrounding purple mist into its body. "Till we meet again," it said, disappearing back into its crystal home.

"You can't just end the story there, Tivan!" exclaimed the Grandmaster.

"I can," the Collector said. "The Time Stone saved the Earth and reasserted itself among the cosmic tapestry. What *more* do you want?"

The Grandmaster thought for a moment. "I wouldn't mind knowing more about that bizarre hatchling," he said. "Do you think it liked me? I felt a vibe."

"Your attention span is sorely lacking, brother. Stay focused."

"I am, I am, I am!" the Grandmaster protested. "Time Stone. *Focused.* Yes."

The Collector returned the dormant crystal to its shelf and returned to his chair. "The Eye of Agamotto still resides on Earth, then," he said somberly. "It's out of our reach."

"You just said *our* reach. Does that mean you're accepting my help?"

"Have you offered it? I can't tell. All you've done is spout nonsense since you've arrived. The Infinity Stones are not a joke. If there is, indeed, one on Knowhere, I want it. If you're interested in joining me on this quest, you'll need to offer up something of value first. I'm afraid your charisma isn't enough. If you have nothing of value, be quiet and stay out of my way." The Collector reached under the cushions of his chair and removed a digital tablet. He moved his finger gently across the screen, activating a holo-numeric touch pad. He dialed a number and was immediately connected to an old friend. "Mizzala? It's Tivan," he said. "I'm in need of your services."

FZZZT!

The tablet sparked as the holographic touch pad

faded in and out. "These older models are infuriating," grumbled the Collector.

"Tivan! What a nice surprise! But you're breaking up, doll. I can't hear you," Mizzala said. "Listen, it's not safe calling me on this line. I've got the Nova Corps on my rear 24/7. Come down to my sideshow. You know where it is. We'll talk in person, catch up. It'll be the bomb diggity."

"I look forward to seeing you, Mizzala," the Collector said magnanimously.

"I know." Mizzala giggled as the transmission ended.

The Grandmaster batted away the touch pad. "Get your devices fixed or upgrade them," he groused. "Anything less is embarrassing."

The Collector was unconcerned with his brother's harsh judgments. His focus was on locating the Stone. "Mizzala is a wealth of information. She'll know something," he said. "She *has* to know something."

"*The bomb diggity?* What does that *mean?*" asked the Grandmaster.

"Mizzala has an obsession with Earth culture. She used to scavenge the wormholes on Sakaar. I'm surprised you never crossed paths. She's consumed with Earth trash. Primitive garbage and paraphernalia from a variety of time periods. Mizzala hoards every piece she can find. A while ago, she relocated here and built a business. Somehow. I'm not exactly sure what she does, but, then again, I'm not entirely interested. She serves her purpose as a contact, and that's enough for me," the Collector declared.

A sparkle appeared in the Grandmaster's eyes. "So which Infinity Stone is here on Knowhere, I wonder, if not the Time Stone? Let's leave this musty old museum and find it. Are you ready to *do this*, brother?"

How can you ask me that question? the Collector thought. *All I've ever wanted to do was find the Stones, you imbecile.*

"Yes." He smirked. "I'm ready to *do this*. Lead the way."

CHAPTER 7

"Come in! Come in!" Mizzala said, clearing a space in her office for the Grandmaster and the Collector. "Have a seat!" She ran to the sofa, picked up a pile of old clothes, and tossed them across a stuffed tiger. The entire space was littered with bizarre antiques, cobbled together from over one hundred years of Earth history. Movie posters. Baseball pennants. Racks of clothing. Outdated technology. She consumed it all. "Sorry about the mess! You know me. I love my *finds*." Mizzala was a tiny woman with a dark complexion and a warm smile. She had a brawny, compact frame. A mass of bright-white braids sat piled atop her head. Mizzala's inviting spirit radiated sweetness. Her office, however, was a complete disaster.

Mizzala ran an underground sideshow and novelty theater. It was a place where people could unwind and enjoy a few hours of pure, galactic strangeness. Though she devoured Earth's oddities, they weren't always easy to come by, seeing as the planet was so far away. Thankfully, plenty of cosmic weirdos were in her sector, so she made do in between those rare and priceless earthly finds. She loved to show them all off. Mizzala hosted comedians, musicians, and artists of all types. Not to mention her crew of regular misfits. There was Nox Dovax, the Man with the Black Hole Belly. He put on a show once a month until someone got sucked into his stomach. People complained after that. Mizzala threw him some cash and told him she'd be in touch after the drama died down. She always took care of her talent.

Glendara was another favorite. She hypnotized her audiences, then sent them out into the universe to perform pranks. A few people ended up in prison after stealing a bunch of stuff from a Nova Corps outpost. Mizzala got into some trouble over

the whole mess. The Nova Corps hadn't quite for-
given her.

The Yooks were a Kree improv troupe. They
weren't very good, but Mizzala admired their passion, so she kept booking them to build their self-
esteem. She was that kind of woman.

The Grandmaster sauntered around the room,
inspecting Mizzala's strange collection. There
were shelves of stuffed animals, glassware, bas-
kets, and children's toys. Piles of records and stacks
of newspapers lined the office's perimeter. "Why
do you have so many things but not display them
properly? What's the point of having curiosities if
you treat them like junk?"

"This is my brother," said the Collector faintly.
"The Grandmaster."

"Get outta here!" Mizzala shouted. "I *thought*
he looked familiar. Well, Grandmaster, you're
known to always be sporting the latest in fashion.
What do you think?" Mizzala asked, twirling in
a circle. She wore a bright neon-red dress with a
high collar. It was roughly two sizes too small. "I

picked it up last week. I don't know what Earth era it's from, but isn't it something?"

"It certainly is," the Grandmaster said, his tone mocking. "Are you sure it isn't a costume of some sort?"

"That's the magic of it! I'm *not* sure. But I love it anyway!" Mizzala exclaimed. Mizzala looked the Grandmaster up and down. "You look hungry. My life partner makes a delicious spiced soup with just a touch of Heat Gel. It's exquisite. Let me have her make you a bowl. It won't take very long to brew up a pot."

"That would be nice," said the Grandmaster, licking his lips.

"There's no time for soup," the Collector said. "Time is of the essence."

She turned her gaze to the Collector, staring at him as though she'd just noticed him. "What a nice surprise it is to see you, Tivan. It's been so long. I don't like your staying all holed up in that museum. Too dark. It's good you're getting out for some fresh air. Or what passes for fresh air on Knowhere."

Mizzala noticed the Grandmaster was carrying a satchel. "What's in the bag? Did you bring a present for me?"

"Unfortunately, no," the Grandmaster said, disappointing Mizzala. "That's something we plan to trade for an Infinity Stone. If such a thing is possible. We're on a quest, you see. My brother tells me you can help us find an Infinity Stone. I was inclined to believe him until we arrived. Now seeing the shoddy state of your quarters, I'm filled with reservations."

Numerous dangerous items surrounded the Collector's feet. Primitive weapons, miniature explosive devices. Some so small they easily fit in his pocket. He plucked a small disk-playing device from the ground and inspected every inch of its design.

"*That's* a Deevee Dee player," Mizzala said, showing him how it worked. "It plays movies. You stick these flimsy little discs in the thingie. Want me to put one on? I've got hundreds. Funny, sad, dramatic. What kinda movies you into?"

"*Focus*, dear," the Collector said, waving his hand to get Mizzala's attention. "There's a rumor one of the Infinity Stones has made it to Knowhere. We need to know its whereabouts."

Mizzala took a tiny gadget out of her pocket. It was a piece of ancient Earth technology, black in color with a small, illuminated screen. She typed out a quick message on the device and shoved it back into the recesses of her dress. "I'll know in a minute."

"What was *that* contraption?" the Grandmaster asked.

"That's my pager. You like it? Earth people used it to communicate, can you believe? I had my tech guy refurbish a whole bunch of them for me. I passed them out to my staff. No one around here even knows they exist, so I've got a private, untraceable network all to myself," Mizzala said. "It's good for secrets, ya know?" She put her arm around the Collector's shoulder. "Speaking of secrets, I hear we buy our treasures from the same guys these days, eh, Tivan? It's almost like we're twins. Don't worry, I won't tell."

The Collector wiggled out of her grasp, insulted. "You accumulate rubbish. I collect valuables. You're charming, Mizzala, there is no doubt. But we are *not* the same."

"Whatever you say, buddy. There's a void inside both of us. Pretending it isn't there doesn't make it go away," Mizzala said knowingly. "My Oobagonian Dream Counselor told me I buy all this stuff to try to fill that void. Maybe she's right? Who knows? Either way, I'm not stoppin'. But enough of that. Let's get back to business. I'm in the middle of hosting a show on the main stage, and I've got only a couple of minutes before I gotta be back. Which Infinity Stone are you looking for? I haven't heard anything about one of them ending up *here*, but, then again, stuff like that isn't my thing. Antique lamps? Those I know a thing or two about."

"I seek the Mind Stone," the Collector said. The brothers had agreed that was the next Stone to focus on, after conceding that searching for the Time Stone would be fruitless. What could be more valuable than the ability to control others' innermost thoughts?

"That one is on Earth, doll," Mizzala said.

"How do *you* know?" asked the Collector.

A wide smirk appeared across Mizzala's face. "Now I get to show you one of my homemade movies!" she crowed, digging through a box on her desk. "It's not like a Deevee Dee. It's *better*." She tossed the box's contents all over the room as she struggled to find what she was looking for.

"*Earth*. Why do items of importance always end up on that backwater planet? Those primitive idiots don't deserve cosmic power. All they do is destroy one another!" the Grandmaster exclaimed. "Though I suppose *everyone* does that. I know I try to destroy someone at least once a week just to stay on top of my game. But humans are so *terrible*."

Mizzala plunked a mechanical cube on her

desk. "You're going to love this!" she shrieked. "I had it made special. It's a hodgepodge of circuits and gizmos. A little bit of everything. I like to know what's happening on Earth. But seeing as it's a long way away, I can't get updates about what's happening as often as I like. So I had my tech guy cobble together all kinds of satellite footage, news reports, secret files, and other clips. He put it all in this here box, added some razzle-dazzle, and now I've got my Earth stories whenever I want 'em. I even added a cute narrator." She pressed a button, and a spritely holographic human appeared. He cheerfully waved at the Collector and the Grandmaster.

"G'day, mates! How *you* doin'?" he asked. "I'm *Jerry*, and I'll be your guide through the crazy world we like to call Earth. What's up with *that*?"

Mizzala clapped her hands in delight. "Gah! I love him. I think you will, too. My tech guy made sure he used all the hip lingo from popular Earth entertainment. Be mindful, though. He's got a glitch or two. I'm working out the kinks." She brought up a menu of options and selected one. "Let's do *New York, New York* first. That'll get you up to speed." She checked her pager. "Nothing on that Infinity Stone yet, but I'll keep you posted." She looked at herself in the mirror. "Time for me to go introduce the next act. Oh! You want Jerry to stop, say *stop*. You want him to pause, say *pause*. *Skip*, *rewind*, *fast-forward*, and so on. You kids have fun. I'll be back shortly." Mizzala scrambled out of the room, leaving the Grandmaster and the Collector alone with the Hologram.

"*Wazzup?!*" Jerry exclaimed.

"Pause!" The Grandmaster looked annoyed. "Where have you brought us, brother?"

"To a place where we can learn all kinds of new information about the Infinity Stones. Be quiet and watch the movie," said the Collector. "*Unpause.*"

"Before we begin, let's meet today's players: the Avengers!" Jerry said, bursting with positive energy. A series of trading card–esque images appeared, showcasing each team member in a variety of action sequences. "First up is Captain

America! Super-soldier Steve Rogers was trapped in a block of ice for decades. And then he wasn't! Now he fights against injustice wherever it hides and is a symbol of freedom for people everywhere."

"What's an America, and why does it require a captain?" asked the Grandmaster. The Collector shushed him.

"Next we've got Iron Man! Tony Stark is one of the most brilliant minds on Earth. A billionaire inventor who created a suit of high-tech armor? Um, I'll take *two*. *Amiright*, ladies?" Jerry said, pretending to raise the roof.

"This is how Earth people *speak*?" asked the Grandmaster incredulously. "If so, I hate them."

"You cats ever hear of a little Asgardian named *Thor*?" Jerry asked.

"Skip!" shouted the Grandmaster.

"And this is the Hulk, also known as Doctor Bruce Banner. Don't make the good doctor *angry*. You wouldn't like him when he's *angry*," Jerry warned, waving his finger in the air.

"Skip!" shouted the Collector.

"Don't skip my Champion!" the Grandmaster protested.

"Black Widow is a super spy named Natasha Romanoff, who takes down her enemies when they aren't looking, which isn't easy because they're *always* looking. As for Clint Barton? He's Hawkeye, a S.H.I.E.L.D. special agent who is quick with a bow and arrow and not much else." Jerry shrugged.

"Gaudy humans," murmured the Grandmaster. *"What are they even avenging?"*

"Everything, silly!" Jerry shouted. The lights dimmed, and the main feature began. A blend of holographic screens appeared, showing a crude patchwork of images. "Our adventure begins with Loki, trickster god of Asgard. That slick hair. That devilish grin. Beware *this* treacherous fellow! He is *rude*."

"Uuuggghhh," the Grandmaster bellowed.

"Loki was cast out of his home on Asgard for being a naughty boy. Oopsie! He was totally desperate for attention. He wanted to hurt his brother

Thor *and* rule the Earth. *Not cool.* So he hooked up with a cosmic bad guy and formed a plan to take his brother down."

"Who? Who was this cosmic *bad guy?*" asked the Collector.

"I don't know, budzilla. I'm just a hologram in a box! *Anyway*, this mysterious baddie wanted something called the Tesseract. What's that? Oh, it's just a little cube that could open up gateways across space. *No big.* The mystery being was *thirsty* for it, so he sent Loki to Earth to go get it. Even loaned him a powerful Scepter that controlled people's minds."

"The Tesseract *and* the Scepter," the Collector mused. "I had no idea."

"The Tesseract contained the Space Stone. One of the six mysterious Infinity Stones. *OoooOooO.* It had fallen into the hands of S.H.I.E.L.D., where Director Nick Fury and his pals had been trying to unlock its secrets for a long time. They enlisted a nutty professor named Doctor Erik Selvig, who worked with S.H.I.E.L.D.'s finest scientists to figure out what that crazy cube could really do! But, if we're being real, it was *way* beyond their level of understanding. One day, everyone was minding their own business when *BOOM!* A portal opened inside the facility where the Tesseract was being kept and *out steps Loki*. He starts attacking Fury's men with the Scepter. *Pew pew! Pew pew!* He's *lovin'* that thing. He's making blasts of cobalt fire and using it to stick people like swine. *Grody*, right? But that's not all the Scepter did. The stone that powered it was called the Mind Stone. One of the six legendary *Infinity Stones*. They're *major*."

"We know," the Grandmaster groaned.

Jerry grinned. "Just checkin'. The Mind Stone is supes cool, especially when it's all snug in the Scepter. Loki used it to control everyone's minds. *Duh.* That's, like, *its favorite thing to do*. First, he controlled Hawkeye, the archer, then Selvig, then a fleet of S.H.I.E.L.D. soldiers. But not Nick Fury. He skedaddled out of there.

"Meanwhile, Loki and his newly brainwashed minions took off. They left that portal high and dry. What happened next? It imploded, of course. The whole facility blew up. Those humans hadn't seen cosmic power like *this* before. Now they had no choice but to assemble a team of enhanced beings to combat this crazy new threat. Enter: the Avengers!" Jerry did a short celebratory dance. "Well, not quite. They don't enter *yet*. But soon!"

The Grandmaster rubbed his hands together in anticipation. "My Champion is going to make an appearance," he said. "*That* will turn this obnoxious tale around."

"Loki found a hiding place and was making his minions do all kinds of dirty work in service of his grand scheme. While they did their thing, he used the Scepter to communicate with a scary-looking guy in another dimension called the Other. He was the middleman between Loki and the mysterious bad guy. Dude looked like a demon! And he wanted that Tesseract for his master. *Bad*. But Loki wasn't about to hand it over until he got what he wanted out the deal: a Chitauri invasion force! *BUM BUM BUM*. The Chitauri were a legion of subservient brutes, ready, willing, and able to die for their master's cause. What did they want in return? *Nothing*. They just love to serve. *Totes cray.*"

"Chitauri are so *easy* to rule. Takes all the fun out of it," the Grandmaster scoffed.

"Loki had to get Doctor Selvig this stuff called Iridium so he could use the Tesseract to open a portal for the Chitauri to invade Earth. *Anyway*. You know my dude Loki, he can't resist a scene. He mind-controlled a bunch of humans *in public*, blabbering about some highfalutin thing, making them kneel before him like he's some big shot. But you'll never guess who showed up to set him straight."

"The Avengers." The Collector sighed.

"THE AVENGERS!" Jerry screamed. "Captain America, Iron Man, and Thor take him down easy peasy. *Or do they?* Loki, that lil' scamp, gave up pretty easily. Pretty, pretty easily. Thor, being a suspicious brother and all, thought he might have a bigger trick up his sleeve. So now the Avengers

have got that sweet Scepter *and* Loki. Even though the god of mischief was trapped in his cell, that didn't mean he was powerless. It was his *job* to manipulate people, so that's what he did. He got these heroes to mistrust one another, sowing seeds of doubt." Jerry tapped the side of his head and grinned like a fool. "Here's the thing. These so-called heroes were barely getting along. Things got hot. Tensions flared. *Hmmmm.* I wonder why. Could it *beeeeee...the Scepter*?! Now that it was in the middle of everything, the Mind Stone was working its magic, pitting the Avengers against one another. They were a time bomb primed to explode. Then Doctor Banner got his hands on the Scepter, and things went nuts. *Tick...tick...tick... BOOM!*"

"Ha! Destroy them all, my Champion!" the Grandmaster exclaimed.

"Um, yeah, that's not what happened." Jerry winced. "What happened is that Hawkeye and his brainwashed buddies showed up to rescue Loki. They attacked the Helicarrier (S.H.I.E.L.D.'s flying-fortress thing that I forgot to mention earlier) and put into motion a series of events that unleashed the power of the Hulk! Who also happened to be Loki's secret weapon. *BOOYAH!* Loki knew how uncontrollable the Hulk really was, but *what he didn't know* was that, despite not being super friends, the Avengers realized they're pretty good at working together. Total miscalc on Loki's part. The Avengers ended up saving the Helicarrier and stopping the Hulk's rampage, but Loki escaped during the chaos. Oh, and he left Hawkeye behind, who was all like, *'What did I just do?! Can someone tell me what just happened?!'* So the Avengers chill for a bit, get a little emo, and decide they're going to get their *you-know-what* together to *Kick. Some. Loki. Butt.*"

"I began this experience with a pronounced sense of dread, but, dare I say, now I'm actually starting to enjoy it," the Grandmaster declared. The Collector remained silent. He was focused on learning as much as he could about the Infinity Stones in question.

"By now, Loki and Doctor Selvig have got the Tesseract hooked up to this crazy contraption that's whizzing and purring at the top of Stark Tower in New York City. All of a sudden, a massive portal opens in the sky, and here comes that Chitauri invading force! Soldiers swarmed. Huge leviathans descended from above. Beast mode in *full effect*. Then the Avengers showed up, and you'll *never* guess what happened next!"

"They won the day. *Obviously*," the Collector said without missing a beat. "What happened to the Scepter and the Tesseract? *Fast-forward* to the end."

Jerry was crestfallen. He didn't get to tell his favorite parts of the story. "Thor took the Tesseract back to Asgard for safekeeping, and S.H.I.E.L.D. got to keep the Scepter." He swiftly regained his energy. "But you'll *really* never guess what happened *next*! Stay tuned for the *Battle of Sokovia*." Jerry froze in an action pose.

"Can you do another one of these, Tivan?" asked the Grandmaster. "I could. I want to kill this hologram, but otherwise, I'm intrigued by these adventures."

"Proceed to the *Battle of Sokovia*, Jerry, but do not bore us with trivial details. Stay focused on the Scepter and the Mind Stone," demanded the Collector.

Jerry jerked back and forth as he recalculated the adventure. "So! S.H.I.E.L.D.'s got that Scepter. They're lookin' at it, checkin' it out and stuff. Then one of their own agents steals it and is like, *'C-YA! I'm going to work for a super-nasty terrorist organization called Hydra now. Byeee!'* He takes it to Wolfgang von Strucker, a Hydra commander who set up a research base in a backwater country called Sokovia. Strucker wanted the Scepter's power so bad! He had Hydra's best scientists working overtime to unlock its secrets. They used its power to energize a handful of recovered Chitauri weapons. It wasn't enough for Strucker, though. He pushed his scientists to experiment on human beings. A lot of Sokovians died. *Sad face.*

But you can't make an omelet without breaking a few eggs, right?"

"How *cruel*," said the Grandmaster. "*True* but *cruel*."

"Then a pair of miraculous young twins broke the cycle of death! Wanda and Pietro Maximoff were granted *enhanced* abilities by the Scepter. Wanda's mind became a magical force of energy. She gained telepathy, telekinesis, and the ability to generate force fields. She could also manipulate a person's mind, creating illusions through her near electric interface. *And* she could levitate!"

"And Pietro?" asked the Grandmaster.

"He could run fast," Jerry answered.

"Poor fellow," the Grandmaster replied.

"Now that Strucker had a little bit of success, his ambition went *off the charts*. He used the Scepter to create an enhanced robot army. Before he knew it, the Avengers got wind of his plans and descended on his fortress. The poor citizens of Sokovia were kind of caught in the cross fire. They just couldn't catch a break! As the Avengers tore through Strucker's troops, Iron Man broke through his base's shields and wandered into Hydra's lab. Turns out, they'd been dissecting one of the enormous Chitauri leviathans, taking its spare parts to create robot drones. Iron Man was so jealous that Strucker got to play with all that cool tech! After he closed his mouth and stopped drooling, Iron Man saw the Scepter, but before he could grab it, Wanda Maximoff worked her magic. The little witch used her power to show Iron Man a terrifying nightmare vision: his teammates destroyed in the cold, desolate reaches of the galaxy! Their cries piercing him like needles! Guilt overwhelming him because he couldn't save their lives! And then it was over. The witch? Gone. *Buh-bye.* All Iron Man could do was shake it off. He grabbed that Scepter and headed home with the Avengers."

"The Mind Stone revealed to him the dark truths deep within," said the Collector. "That's what it does. *Continue.*"

"Yeah! Totally, man," Jerry said, nodding his

head in agreement. "Um, yeah, so Iron Man scrutinized that Scepter like an animal. He just couldn't figure that crazy thing out! Then he realized that the Scepter was just a casing used to contain the power of the Mind Stone. Total lightbulb moment. Stark was like, *'Ya know what? I'm def using the Scepter's energy to fuel the Ultron peacekeeping program I've been working on in secret.'* Banner knew what he was up to since they're science bros, but the rest of the Avengers were *totes* in the dark. Stark didn't like lying to them, but *whatever.* What's a little fib if it means he can achieve global peace?! The whole experience drained him. His brain hurt; he didn't sleep. Just when he thought he'd reached a breaking point, Ultron awakened! All thanks to the snazzy Mind Stone, which, it turns out, was *not* a good thing. Ultron strangled Stark's J.A.R.V.I.S. program, cobbled together a body made of discarded parts, and surprised the Avengers while they were trying to party! He took control of Stark's Iron Legion and made them attack everyone! Nice introduction. *Not.* And it was *just the beginning*. Ultron wanted to destroy the whole planet, so he disappeared into the web, and eventually found himself in Strucker's lab, surrounded by all that exotic Chitauri weaponry."

"Where did the Scepter go?" asked the Collector.

"Ultron snagged it. The Avengers were *miffed*. Now Ultron is all plottin' to wipe humanity off the face of the Earth. He even drafted those nutty twins to help him execute his plans. He promised them all kinds of stuff he wasn't going to deliver. They followed him cuz, well, they'd been stranded and abused. They didn't have anyone else."

The Grandmaster nudged his brother. "Kind of like your little Keelan, Tivan," he said.

"Ultron was ready to get this show on the road, but first he needed to steal this awesome metal called vibranium. He went after it, the Avengers showed up, it was a real scene. But! During the battle, Wanda the Witch worked her magic on our heroes. She put each of them into a trance and showed them all sorts of scary visions and fractured realities. Destruction. Pain. Death. She even got into the Hulk's head and used him as a weapon against Iron Man."

"I'd have charged an arm and a leg for a contest like that," the Grandmaster said. "*So many* arms and legs."

"These visions. I want to know what they mean," said the Collector.

"So did Thor!" exclaimed Jerry. "They really scared the bejabbers out of him. He thought they were actual visions of *the future*, so he took a bath in this little cave hot tub called the Water of Sights, and that's where he saw them—*the Infinity Stones*! But we'll come back to the other ones in a moment. In the meantime, Ultron had used the Scepter to fuel a brand-new body for himself, but before it fully energized, the Avengers stole it. And the twins? *Waaay* in over their heads. When they realized Ultron wasn't planning to keep them around much longer, they bolted and joined the Avengers, who were all like, *'Welcome to the team, buddies!'*" Jerry's endless storytelling stopped cold, and he became extremely sad. "I wish *I* had buddies." He quickly snapped out of his funk. "Keep it together, Jerry!" he exclaimed. "Where was I? *OH YEAH*. Stark uploaded his own AI program into the robot body with the help of J.A.R.V.I.S. Cue lots of arguing with his teammates. Thor delivered an Asgardian-size jolt of power to that swanky android, and a brand-new being was born! *The Vision*. Smack dab in the middle of his forehead was the Mind Stone. Without the Vision, no way were the Avengers going to defeat Ultron. The dude knew what was up! He even lifted Thor's hammer."

"Tivan, you said something like that wasn't possible!" the Grandmaster exclaimed.

"All things are possible with the Infinity Stones. Pipe down so we can get this over with," the Collector scolded. "*Fast-forward* to the end."

"The Avengers saved the planet. Ultron was like, '!,' but Vision was like, '*Oh no, you didn't!*' and vaporized him with the Mind Stone," Jerry said. "When the dust settled, the Avengers were like, '*Uh, what just happened?*' Iron Man needed a major nap, so he peaced out. Thor couldn't get those crazy visions out of his head, so he took off into space to find the other Infinity Stones."

"Pause!" the Collector shouted. He turned to the Grandmaster, glaring. *"You didn't tell me this."*

"Well, he certainly wasn't looking for them when he was on Sakaar. He was too busy trying to escape my clutches. I've got *very* sharp clutches," said the Grandmaster. "What happened to the twins, Jerry?"

"Pietro died, and Wanda became an Avenger called the Scarlet Witch. Captain America also drafted War Machine, Falcon, and Vision. The whole team leveled up after Sokovia!" said Jerry. "But you'll *really* never guess what happened *next*! Stay tuned for *The Sokovia Accords* and *Return of the Winter Soldier*." Jerry froze in yet another action pose.

The Collector had become antsy. "Tell us what happened to the Mind Stone and be done with it," he groused. "I have become impatient."

Jerry jolted back and forth as he reprogrammed

himself. "Vision learned how to be human despite his being an artificial intelligence. For all his smarts, he had no idea that the Infinity Stone that gave him life was one of the most powerful and sought-after things in all existence! Total mystery to him. Well, not *total*. *OH!* He also got flirty with Wanda. *On the DL*. It didn't work out so well. Wanda ended up using her connection to the Mind Stone to help overpower Vision in an act of defiance. There was a whole Super Hero civil war thing. You probably don't want to hear about it."

"That is correct. *End*," said the Collector. "Now summon Mizzala. We've no more time for these stories. If she doesn't have the information we need, we'll seek it elsewhere."

Jerry's tone grew somber. He appeared to be overwhelmed with emotion. "Can you take me with you? Please?" he asked. "Some tech dude altered my algorithms and trapped me inside this cube. You think I *want* to sound like this? I'm trapped in here. I used to be a robot, man. I need help. Do me a solid?"

The Grandmaster grabbed a mallet from the floor and smashed the mechanical cube to bits.

"What have you done?!" barked the Collector.

"I put that poor, annoying thing out of its misery," the Grandmaster said. "Don't tell me you actually felt sorry for the little hologram man."

WEEEOOO! WEEEOOO! WEEEOOO!

Sirens rang out as Mizzala rushed into the room. She had a panicked look on her face. "We've got a problem," she said, struggling to catch her breath. "Technically, I've done a few illegal things over the years. I'm not proud but, you know."

"Out with it!" the Grandmaster exclaimed.

"The Nova Corps is here, and they're taking everyone to jail," she said. "It happens."

"What luck. Tivan pays people in Nova Corps to stay out of his business. He can help smooth it all out for you. Tell her," the Grandmaster said, jostling his brother.

"That was a lie," the Collector admitted. "Never speak of it again."

Mizzala's pager vibrated. *"Cleeton's Retreat!"* she

exclaimed. "*That's* the place you need to go to find out about the Infinity Stone." The sound of approaching Nova Corpsmen grew louder. Mizzala kicked away a pile of old shoes to reveal a trapdoor. "I'll deal with these turkeys. You two need to hightail it. Get in here. It'll take you somewhere safe, don't worry."

"What is it?" the Collector asked.

Mizzala struggled to get the words out. She knew they wouldn't be well received. "It's a sewage chute. *Sorry*," she said, pushing the brothers through the trapdoor to freedom.

CHAPTER 8

The Grandmaster and the Collector had been walking for over an hour. Their clothes were caked in muck. The sewage chute had spat them out in an unfamiliar location. That didn't sit well with the Collector. He'd been under the impression he knew every inch of Knowhere. Slogging through the planetoid's most impoverished areas, he realized this impression was incorrect. The ugliest side of Knowhere had seemingly escaped his view. It was something he would address at a later date. His current focus was on locating that Infinity Stone.

"Time is running out, brother," the Grandmaster reminded him. "We've taken so long; some other cosmic despot probably has the Infinity Stone by now. All this for nothing. Ugh! I can't think about it. How close are we to Cleeton's Retreat?" The Collector remained conspicuously silent. "Oh no. No, no, no. Do you even know where this place is, Tivan?!"

"I was unaware of its existence until today," the Collector said softly.

The Grandmaster steamed. "*How?* How is that possible?" He pointed to a rusty billboard, plastered on the side of a nearby housing pod. "That says the Tivan Group! Your grubby fingers are all over this husk of a planetoid. Explain to me how you don't know where things are?!"

"I've been busy!" the Collector snapped. But that wasn't it at all—quite the opposite, in fact. He'd realized it must have sprung up sometime after the tragedy. He really needed to get out more.

"Busy neglecting your duties," the Grandmaster needled, as though he'd read the Collector's mind. "If you want to rule, you're going to need to remove yourself from that putrid chair and *notice your surroundings*!"

The Collector took a deep, calming breath. "I'm doing *just that*," he growled.

"Knowhere teems with filth. The smell is rancid. The air is thick and toxic. As I prepared for my visit, I knew I'd encounter all these things, but I had no idea I'd actually end up *covered in waste*," the Grandmaster said with despair. The Collector almost felt bad for his brother. Almost. "On Sakaar, I was a respected figurehead. Feared by many. Hated by some. Loved by few, depending. I hadn't just built a business, I built an empire. I was *someone*."

"And now you're not," the Collector said flatly. "Things change. Get over it." He spotted a corridor ahead where a broken pipe gushed water. It was next to an exhaust vent that spewed a hot stream of polluted air. "There. We'll wash and dry ourselves."

"I'm not doing that," the Grandmaster refused.

"You needn't *undress*," the Collector assured him.

"Bathing in the street is something poor people do," the Grandmaster snarled. "I am not a poor person! I'm a galactic icon!"

The Collector grabbed his brother by his collar. "You lost your station! You lost your kingdom! It's all been destroyed, En Dwi! Adapt or die, it makes no difference to me, but either stay the course or *stay out of my way*."

The Grandmaster grinned. "There's some fire inside you, after all," he said, removing his brother's hand. "Don't touch me again, or I'll rip your fingers off, one by one, and feed them to that Xandarian Boulder-Crusher you keep in your basement, *brother*." He stormed over to the cascade of water and began to clean the sludge off his golden robe. "This is so humiliating," he moaned, splashing water across his body, scouring every dirty inch. The Collector watched him for a moment before joining. Once clean, the brothers stood in front of the exhaust vent and let the powerful air currents dry them. It felt good in a strange way, as long as they didn't think for too long about what was actually happening. Once finished, they continued on their way.

They passed a small beggar child on the street. His hand was outstretched, waiting for someone to place a coin in it. The Grandmaster knelt down to address him. "Hello, little one. We are looking for a venue called Cleeton's Retreat. Do you know where it might be?" he asked. The boy pointed to his empty hand. The Grandmaster pushed it away. "Get your rancid palm out of my face and answer the question."

"Shove it up your nasal cavity, twig!" the boy barked.

"I should put you in a labor camp. Ungrateful little animal," the Grandmaster snarled.

A fleet of Nova Corpsmen was headed their way, spreading out across the area. The brothers needed to hide.

"There," the Collector said, pointing to a dark area under a bridge. It was filled with outcasts, wanderers, and vagabonds. "They won't search a place like that. We'll be safe." They rushed into the park and lingered among its inhabitants. They were desperate to blend in or face capture.

"Why are *we* hiding from the Nova Corps?" asked the Grandmaster. "We've done nothing wrong. We were merely in the wrong place at the wrong time."

"Have you not killed? Have you not stolen?" the Collector replied. "The Nova Corps turns a blind eye when we do our dirty work within the confines of our homes, but we're out in the open now. We can't take any risks. Stay silent, be humble, and remain patient."

The brothers strolled under the bridge, watching people go about their daily business. Some of them made food and shared it with friends and family. Some entertained one another with jokes. Others played games to pass the time.

"Look, Tivan. Those people are playing Astro Chips," the Grandmaster said, pointing. "Do you remember when we used to play that game as younglings? I used to beat you. A lot. You'd get so furious you'd try to stab me." The Grandmaster sighed contentedly, looking wistful. "Ah, such fun memories."

"I've forgotten my childhood," replied the Collector. The statement wasn't entirely true. Many of his youthful memories had faded, but not all. He always remembered the colored lights in the sky. The ones that kept him up at night. They came to him in dreams. Red, blue, green, purple, yellow, and orange ingots. Some days he'd see them everywhere he looked. He couldn't get them out of his mind. It wasn't until he grew to adulthood that he realized what they truly were and set forth to collect them. Now he found himself close to one, yet again, and the thought infused him with hope.

The Grandmaster saw his brother growing starry-eyed and knew exactly what he was thinking about. "You've forgotten everything except your love of the Infinity Stones, is that it?" asked the Grandmaster. "You really are controlled by those little rocks."

"I'm controlled by nothing!" the Collector shot

back. He knew the words were a lie as soon as they left his lips. The Infinity Stones *did* control him, but he wasn't about to give his brother any more ammunition.

"Answer me this," the Grandmaster said. "What would you do to secure the Infinity Stones?"

The Collector didn't waste any time answering. *"Anything."*

"Good. Because if we find ourselves confronted with a hard choice, I will hold you to that statement. And, for the record, the Infinity Stones *totally* control you. I find it endlessly humorous."

The brothers' feet were sore and aching. They took a seat on a bench next to a derelict couple in the middle of a heated argument. Though the commotion annoyed the brothers, the bench was the only place to sit in the entire park. They shamelessly listened in on the couple's conversation.

"I'm tired of running, Taago!" the woman exclaimed. "Better that we face the mistakes of our past than continue in this life. Look at us. Sitting in a beggars' park, eating scraps. I'm tired of hiding in the shadows. We need to face reality!"

The man named Taago shook his head back and forth. "You're not thinking straight, Bel. We need hide out only a little longer. Till things settle down. Then we can join our children off-world. If we try to leave now, Nartaz will find us, and it'll all be over."

The Grandmaster interrupted the couple's conversation. "Sorry, but did you just say *Nartaz*?"

Bel nodded. "Yes," she said. "He's here to collect his bounty and be gone. That's the way of the Ravagers. What of it?"

"And he's collecting a bounty on *you*?" the Grandmaster asked.

Taago eyed him with suspicion. "Who are you?" he asked. "You're one of Nartaz's Ravager friends, aren't you?" Taago grabbed the Grandmaster, tossed him to the ground in anger, and held a foot to his throat. "Scream and I'll crush your windpipe."

The threat made the Grandmaster laugh—well, more like a cough. "Hahahaha! Oh, this is wonderful. What a pleasant surprise. It feels good to see some viciousness around here, even if it is directed toward me. If you weren't a stinking derelict, I'd offer you a job. Now let me up before I linger on this moment and become angry."

"Forgive my brother, sir," the Collector pleaded. "He pokes his nose where it shouldn't be. We are not in cahoots with this Nartaz, I assure you."

"Look at us," the Grandmaster demanded. "Do we *look* like Ravagers?!"

Taago stared down at the Grandmaster for a moment, and then shrugged. He released the Grandmaster and helped him to his feet.

"I'm hungry, too, by the way. We're not *all* that different," the Grandmaster said, dusting himself off. He leaned in close to Taago and looked him dead in the eye. "If I ever see you again after I leave this cesspool, the result won't be pretty." He leaned in even closer and whispered in Taago's ear. "I'll decapitate you in front of your mate, send the head to your offspring, and chop the rest up for animal

food." Taago, trembling, backed away in fear. A pleasing sight to the Grandmaster. "Brother, let's leave these nice people alone and be on our way, *hmm*?" The brothers nodded farewell, noticing that the Nova Corps had cleared out of the park. "Back on track at last! Let's get out of this pit of despair. Once we secure this Infinity Stone, we'll need to find a suitable containment device for it. I'm thinking a belt might be nice."

"Is this Nartaz a friend of yours?" the Collector asked.

"No. I was simply being nosy," the Grandmaster said. "I appreciate your subtle and surprising act of heroism. I didn't know you had it in you. Inspired to be an Avenger? I noticed how enamored you were by that obnoxious holographic presentation. Bewitched by the Avengers and their antics."

"I'm simply fascinated that a team of enhanced humans—*ants* by any cosmic standard—have somehow found themselves swept up in matters of the universe. They're meddlesome. I wish they would stay on Earth and mind their own business."

"I think you're jealous. You want to *be* a hero, don't you?"

"I want to *rule*," the Collector clarified. "The Infinity Stones will give me the power to do it. I won't be questioned on the matter any further."

But the Grandmaster was not taking the hint. "You, rule?" He sneered. "With what, Tivan? I know you don't have the Aether. It was clear to me as soon as you told me you possessed the thing. If you truly had it, you'd use it. Any sane being knows, if you have a cosmic weapon, you unleash it upon whomever you need to get whatever it is you want." He lowered his voice. "If you lost the Aether during the *incident*, just tell me. I'm sure it fills you with shame to have had your hands on two of the Infinity Stones, only to watch them yanked away by twists of fate."

The Collector felt cornered and embarrassed. *"I have nothing to prove to you,"* he said through gritted teeth.

The Grandmaster patted his arm. "Now, now. Just because you're at the weakest point doesn't mean you can't rise again. You don't see me sulking around my husk of a menagerie, yelling at my underling, drooling all over myself. *Get yourself together, Tivan.* We have work to do. An Infinity Stone awaits! But where the devil is Cleeton's Retreat?!" the Grandmaster exclaimed to no one in particular. The parkgoers all pointed in the exact same direction. Toward a large, glowing sign in the distance that said CLEETON'S RETREAT. "Oh. Well, I'm not sure how we missed that," he said. "Let's be on our way."

CHAPTER 9

"Hello. I am the Grandmaster, and this is my brother, the Collector. We are looking for Cleeton. Would you mind showing us to his table? The matter is very important."

The hostess was starstruck by the surprise arrival. "It's *YOU*!" she exclaimed, pointing at the Grandmaster. "The Exalted Overseer is going to lose his mind! *Wait right here*." She dashed away, waving her arms excitedly and giggling to herself.

"What kind of egotistical maniac calls himself the *Exalted Overseer*?" the Grandmaster asked. "Shall we take a look?" He waved his brother over, and together they peeked their heads into an enormous space. It was a mesmerizing and strange sight. The outdated décor was exclusively gold.

Tacky paintings covered the walls. They looked to be the scribbles of a child. An expansive and brightly lit dance floor sat completely bare of occupants excepting a few random aliens laid across the floor, sleeping deeply.

"What *is* this place?" asked the Grandmaster.

The hostess returned quickly. She couldn't contain her excitement. "Mr. Grandmaster, Mr. Collector, may I present to you my boss and the son of this establishment's owner?" The hostess giggled. "The Exalted Overseer!"

A short green man, covered in gold jewelry, rounded the corner, high-fiving the air as he jogged. He wore a loose-fitting frock, a voluminous cape, and an oversize turban. It was as if he had discovered a trunk full of costumes and put them all on at once. His behavior was immature and spontaneous. It wasn't clear if he was a man-size child or a child-size man. The Collector and the Grandmaster shared a glance in a rare moment of camaraderie, prepared for the worst.

"Yayayayayaya, the Grandmaster is in *the shed*!"

the Exalted Overseer shouted. He grabbed the Grandmaster and hugged him tightly. "I've been dreaming of this day since I was a teensy, lil' spud. Just being *near you* gives me the tingle tangles. Now that you're here, I'm going to make you one of my closest *zangos*."

"A pleasure," the Grandmaster said, pushing the Exalted Overseer away. "I'm flattered to be here in *'the shed'* and honored to be made a *'zango.'* Whatever those things might be."

"A *zango* is like a buddy, and *the shed* is wherever I'm partying. I make up words. *Cuz I'm a genius like dat*," the Exalted Overseer said, pursing his lips. "Everybody says I'm really good at it. Sometimes I just say whatever is on my mind! Even if it doesn't make any sense!" His tone shifted from cheerful to pure evil in an instant. *"This is my domain. You play by my rules here. Remember that."* The Exalted Overseer walked the brothers through the empty club to a large, private area in the rear. It was filled with long, luxurious couches that looked like beds. Tables overflowed with exotic finger foods. Four potbellied, alien body-guards flanked EO's table, which was nestled in the corner of the dimly lit room.

"*Spiced Slug Larva* and *Phelch Juice*," the Grandmaster gasped. He ran to the food and began stuffing his face as methodically as possible. The Exalted Overseer hovered next to him, clearly in awe of his every move.

"You have no idea what it means to me that you came here," the Exalted Overseer gushed. "I'm, like, *your biggest fan in the whole galaxy*. You're my hero. I *love* the way you crush people. I'm gonna run a Contest of Champions, too, someday. It'll be so *buhgock*! That means *cool*."

"Who's Cleeton?" the Grandmaster asked, his mouth full of snacks.

"That's my pippity-pap. My dad," the Exalted Overseer said. "He owns this place. Gave it to me for my birthday so my zangos and I had a place to chill. I don't let anyone else in."

"How do you make any money?" asked the Grandmaster.

"Hahahahahaha! I don't need to make money. My family is rich!" the Exalted Overseer cackled wildly. When he saw his bodyguards weren't laughing, he laughed harder, glaring at them in silent instruction to join in. Reluctantly, they did. "That's right! You laugh when I laugh!" he screamed at the top of his lungs. "I'm the boss!"

The Grandmaster was nonplussed by the Exalted Overseer's tantrum but impressed with how his minions obeyed their master's orders. "You have quite a command over your employees," he remarked. "Their bodies are too gelatinous for my needs, but I like their style."

"You like *my* style, zaddy?" the Exalted Overseer asked, giving a turn and showing off his bizarre outfit. The Grandmaster stared at him blankly.

"We're here to speak to you about an Infinity Stone, Exalted Overseer," the Collector cut in abruptly. "It's come to our attention that you're in possession of one. We're interested in seeing it."

The Exalted Overseer lay down on his long white couch and relaxed. "Cool, cool," he said with a smile. "I'm really into the Infinity Stones. Gotta grab 'em all, right?! But before we talk business, I want you to tell me a story."

"A story?" replied the Collector.

"Did I stutter, old man?" the Exalted Overseer growled. His tone turned dark and spiteful. "I *want* a story, I *get* a story. That's how it goes around here. I'm the Exalted Overseer, dung cave. When you're in *my* roost, you play by *my* rules. Now. *Do you know any good stories?*"

"He knows many," the Grandmaster said, stuffing another Spiced Slug Larva into his mouth. "Tell the boy a story, Tivan. We're in his roost."

"I'M NOT A BOY!" the Exalted Overseer protested. "I'm a *young man.*"

The Collector had to be careful. The Exalted Overseer was clearly unstable. This wouldn't be a simple transaction. To see whether he was actually in possession of the Infinity Stone, the Collector had to play by his enemy's strange rules. Such a thing required a level of patience the Collector wasn't sure he had. *Remember the quest, Tivan*, he thought. *You're close to retrieving your prize. Stay the course.* "Young man, since you're such a fan of the Infinity Stones, do you want to know a story about the Power Stone?" he asked.

The Exalted Overseer clapped his hands together and wiggled around in his seat. "Yes, yes, yes. Tell me. No, don't! Wait. No, tell me!" he exclaimed.

The Collector took a deep breath to calm himself and sat alongside this crazy individual. "Have you heard of the Guardians of the Galaxy?" he asked, giving an involuntary shudder. Just saying the name out loud made his skin crawl.

"*DUH!* I'm Star-Lord's number-one fan," said the Exalted Overseer. He called out to the Grandmaster, who had just chugged a glass of Phelch Juice. "Don't worry, my zango, I'm still your biggest fan, too!"

The Grandmaster paused his feasting and leaned down to his brother's ear. "Do you truly know the *whole* version of whatever story you're about to tell?" he asked. "If you don't, this may not end well for us."

"I lived it," the Collector replied.

The Exalted Overseer snapped his fingers. His four bodyguards surrounded him with pillows. He settled in and got comfortable. "I want you to tell the story *really good*."

The Collector took a deep, calming breath. "The tale begins on the planet Morag, where a Terran man named Peter Quill found the mysterious Orb among the planet's rocky terrain. Before he could safely retrieve it, he was ambushed by Korath, a Kree hunter. The Orb was in high demand, you see. Korath and his lackeys battled Quill, who escaped with the Orb, but just barely."

"Stop calling him Quill! His name is *Star-Lord*," whined the Exalted Overseer. He narrowed his eyes. "You're not very good at telling stories."

This boy tries my patience, the Collector thought. *But I must stay calm.* He nodded and continued.

"Korath, defeated, returned to deliver the bad

news to his superior, the Kree terrorist known as Ronan. It was not well received. Ronan was charged with securing the Orb, not for himself but for a third party."

"Yeah. *Thanos.* You mean *Thanos*," EO said.

"Who?" asked the Collector. The name threw him off balance. He'd heard it before, of course, many times. Thanos was a fearsome cosmic warlord whose name caused entire worlds to shiver in fright. But the Collector hadn't heard the revelation that it was Thanos who sought the Orb. He remained coy and made a mental note to investigate further.

"*Thanos* is the guy who hired Ronan," the Exalted Overseer snarled. "Keep telling the story!"

"Of course," the Collector said, regaining his composure. "Ronan sought to destroy Xandar and, apparently, Thanos was the one who'd help him do it. But only once he received the Orb. The Kree and Xandarians were longtime enemies. Now that the Orb was in Star-Lord's hands, there was a question as to whether Ronan would be able to deliver on his promise. Gamora, a deadly assassin, and one of Ronan's minions, volunteered to steal the Orb from Star-Lord and bring it back for her master."

"Gamora is Thanos's daughter," said the Exalted Overseer. "*Duh.* You are such a dum-dum!"

One day I will watch the flesh peel from your bones, you stupid little ingrate! the Collector thought.

"Star-Lord met with the Broker on Xandar, hoping to sell the Orb for a hefty price. He had no such luck. Once Star-Lord mentioned his run-in with the Kree, the Broker, in his infinite wisdom, wanted no part of something a vile man like Ronan was after. He shooed Quill—I mean, *Star-Lord*—out of his shop and into the path of Gamora, who swiftly snatched the Orb from his grasp. Then a pair of bizarre creatures became involved after noting a pricey bounty on Star-Lord's head."

"Rocket and Groot to the rescue!" the Exalted Overseer chimed in. He jumped onto the cushions and pretended to act out an action-packed scene.

The Collector turned to his brother with a

puzzled look on his face. The Exalted Overseer seemed to know more than he was letting on.

"Tell our friend what happened next, brother," the Grandmaster pressed, with a slight shake of his head.

"They raced across Xandar to retrieve the Orb until the Nova Corps interfered. They confiscated the Orb, arrested Star-Lord, Gamora, and the two creatures, then sent them to the Kyln prison colony to rot. The Kyln was filled with vicious criminals. While incarcerated, the group realized they had more in common than they originally thought. Now joined by a gentleman named Drax the Destroyer, they broke out of the Kyln, retrieved the Orb, and were on their way to Knowhere to sell it." The Collector drew a steadying breath. This is where things got really painful. *"To me."*

"I bet Ronan was angry about that," said the Exalted Overseer.

"Indeed. So angry that he killed his benefactor's messenger out of spite, a creature called the Other," the Collector said. His eyes widened in excitement as soon as he heard himself say the words. Pieces of a grand cosmic puzzle had suddenly come together in a way he didn't expect. "The Other!" he exclaimed, turning to the Grandmaster. "Ronan killed the Other. The same person Loki did business with during that whole thing on Earth. That means Thanos was the one who hired Loki to retrieve the Tesseract from Earth. Thanos had possession of the Scepter as well. Don't you see?! It's all coming together now! Thanos is after the Infinity Stones!"

The Exalted Overseer angrily tossed a pillow in the Collector's direction. *"STOP GOING OFF TRACK!"* he screeched. *"TELL THE STORY!"*

The Collector caught the pillow and placed it on the ground beside him. Boiling rage had crept into his body. He struggled desperately to contain it. *Keep it together, Tivan*, he thought. *This child may be a bigger resource than you imagine. Stay patient. Use him. Do not lose control.* "Where was I? Oh yes. Star-Lord and his friends had the Orb at last but were unaware of its immense power."

"A recurring theme, you'll find!" chimed in the Grandmaster.

"They headed to my museum here on Knowhere to sell the Orb. When they arrived on my doorstep, I was unsure as to whether they were serious players. To me, they seemed ignorant and inferior. But they possessed something I wanted very much, so I did business with them. It's a familiar situation that I find myself in more often than I'd like. However, I do what I need to do to get what I want. These so-called Guardians required a lesson on the Infinity Stones, so I gave them one. They learned that what they had in their possession was no ordinary Orb; it was the Power Stone. An item capable of infusing its owner with galactic dominance and the ability to cause mass destruction. Oh, *the beauty*." The Collector found himself getting worked up as he recounted the tale. "And then my petty, idiotic, substandard slave ripped the Power Stone from the Orb, unleashing its raw energy on my museum, tearing it apart inch by inch. A lifetime's worth of work destroyed in an instant. My whole world crashed down around me. I haven't been the same since." A sense of relief swept over the Collector's body. Sharing this most personal and difficult tale with the Exalted Overseer had, strangely enough, given him some peace of mind.

"And then?" the Exalted Overseer whispered with bated breath.

"While I was indisposed, the Guardians took the Orb and, with it, the Power Stone," the Collector said.

"Javen's Nuggs, that is *frothy*!" exclaimed the Exalted Overseer.

The Collector mustered a fake smile, nodding at the young man in agreement. "Yes. Very *frothy*. That's the exact word I would use to describe the experience. It's no wonder you've accomplished so much in your short life with a vocabulary so colorful."

"Oh yeah. I'm real smart. I know all the best words," said the Exalted Overseer. "Hey. I heard

Gamora fell in love with Star-Lord. Is that true? I heard they kissed. Did they kiss? Sometimes I like to pretend I'm Star-Lord and my pillow is Gamora, and I kiss my pillow."

The Grandmaster saw his brother getting agitated once more and stepped in to steer the conversation back on course. "Let's return to our exciting adventure, shall we?" he offered.

The Collector regained his composure. "I will give you the abbreviated version, and then we will move on to business," he said firmly. "Ronan wrestled the Power Stone away from the Guardians. He finally had the ability to destroy Xandar himself and set out to do it without the aid of his master. He opened the Orb and was instantly intoxicated. He smashed the Stone onto his Cosmi-Rod—quite a stupid name for a weapon, if you ask me—and invaded Xandar with his ship, the *Dark Aster*, and a fleet of Necro-Craft by his side. The Nova Corps, who'd now teamed up with the Guardians, formed a planetary blockade with their Star Blasters, which Ronan tore apart with ease. Star-Lord and his friends boarded the *Dark Aster* and tried to stop Ronan with a very powerful weapon. Their plan failed. The Power Stone's energy protected Ronan completely. Feeling unstoppable, he descended to the surface of Xandar to enact his final revenge as the Guardians followed behind."

"And then, to win the day, Star-Lord distracted Ronan with song and dance!" the Exalted Overseer interrupted. He hopped to his feet and began to gyrate in the awkward silence.

"If you *know* this story, then why are you making me tell it?!" barked the Collector.

The Exalted Overseer stopped dancing, got down from his perch, and put his face close to the Collector's. "Because *I'm* in control." His tone was light and playful, but behind it lurked a streak of pure, soulless hate. "You do what *I* say, and I *might* give you what you want. Finish the story. You're almost done."

The Collector grinned and continued. "When Ronan's Cosmi-Rod shattered, Star-Lord was almost destroyed by the raw energy of the Power

Stone, but his allies grabbed hold of one another and used their bodies to vaporize Ronan instead. Star-Lord handed the Stone over to the Nova Corps for safekeeping, so they expunged the Guardians' criminal records and left them with a warning to stay out of trouble," the Collector said. *"The end."*

"You left out a few parts," the Exalted Overseer said with a smirk. "About Yondu and the Ravagers. But whatever. Ravagers are weird."

"How do *you* know all this?" the Grandmaster asked.

"I told you, I'm rich. I pay all kinds of people to tell me stuff. I never know if it's true or not," the Exalted Overseer revealed. "Just a heads up, the Nova Corps doesn't have the Power Stone any longer. I know that for sure. Thanos has it. *That's* a story I haven't heard. Asked all my informants, but no one seems to know the juice. Do you?"

The Grandmaster filled with excitement. *"Oh. We know the juice,"* he said. "Don't we know the juice, brother?" He leaned in to the Collector's ear once more. "Give him something good so he'll give us that Infinity Stone. I know you can taste it just as much as I can."

"I know all the juice," the Collector said with a roll of his eyes. He was desperate to end the interaction. "The Nova Corps isn't qualified to store an item like the Power Stone. They're a sad organization run by fools and imbeciles. Nova Prime is a preening, egotistical zealot who hires substandard Corpsmen. They're barely qualified to wipe their own backsides. They have no business interfering in galactic matters."

The Grandmaster nudged his brother. "Yes, but *the juice*," he said. "How did this Thanos person, the one you *knew* existed but didn't *really* know existed, get the Power Stone?"

"Oh." The Collector struggled to come up with something. He hadn't heard a single thing about the incident in question. His depression kept him slightly behind on recent matters. An idea formed in his brain. He knew exactly the type of story that would keep the Exalted Overseer engaged. "Star-Lord stole it for Thanos," he said. "Yes. That's it."

"*WOO-HOO!*" screamed the Exalted Overseer. "*STAR-LORD FOREVER!*"

The Collector was on a roll. His lie quickly took shape. "Star-Lord and his zangos had been roaming the galaxy looking for trouble when, all of a sudden, Thanos called. He wanted that Power Stone and knew just the man to take it."

The Exalted Overseer's eyes lit up. He could hardly contain his excitement.

"To complete his mission, Star-Lord left the Guardians behind and went deep undercover inside the Nova Corps. But he needed help to hatch his plan, so he drafted a crafty *young man*, the son of an abandoned-club owner, who trained him, guided him, and taught him how to be a hero. Star-Lord trusted this rich, well-dressed genius more than anyone else in the universe. Together they crushed a battalion of Nova Corpsmen, liberated the Power Stone, and bequeathed it to Thanos, who celebrated their victory with a feast," the Collector said. He watched as the Exalted Overseer clasped his hands together, anxious for a triumphant finale. "After an evening of revelry, Star-Lord and his companion returned home, where *Gamora* was waiting. She was impressed by their achievements. Bored by Star-Lord, she grabbed the young man and kissed him passionately in front of *all his friends*."

The Grandmaster couldn't help but double over in laughter. "Hahahaha! What an incredible tale!" he cackled. "I'd make you tell it again if we weren't pressed for time. Was that or was that not satisfying, Exalted Overseer?"

"Sure was," the Exalted Overseer said with a smile.

"Then show us the Infinity Stone," growled the Grandmaster, suddenly switching tactics.

The Exalted Overseer snapped his fingers, and one of his bodyguards brought over a metal box.

He lifted the lid, showing off what was inside. It was a glowing orange rock. "This is the Soul Stone. *Frothy*, right?" he said. "Look, but don't touch."

The Collector eyed the rock with suspicion. He was under the impression that the Soul Stone was either lost or under the care of someone much more powerful. Regardless, he wanted it. He couldn't risk the opportunity. The Collector reached into his brother's satchel and pulled out an item to trade. "This is a Wishing Ore," he said. "Crack it. I imagine you'll like what's inside."

"It's ugly and boring," the Exalted Overseer remarked. He grabbed the rock and threw it against the wall, breaking it in half. A tiny, lizard-like fairy exploded from inside. It flew in circles, dizzy from the experience. The Exalted Overseer held out his hand, and the fairy landed on his palm. *"Wow,"* he gasped.

"Go ahead, wise one," said the Grandmaster. "Make a wish."

The Exalted Overseer violently clapped his hands together and smashed the fairy, destroying it in an instant. The creature's orange innards splashed in all directions. "Everyone knows a Wishing Ore fairy is filled with rainbow sparkles. *This* is a fake," he said. "And I don't like fakes." The young man moved to grab the Grandmaster, but the Collector grabbed his arm and stopped him.

"That would be a very poor choice," said the Collector, tossing away the Exalted Overseer's arm.

The Grandmaster swiped the alleged Soul Stone from its box. Glowing orange paint wiped off on the palm of his hand. "*We* don't like fakes, either," he said. The Exalted Overseer's bodyguards slowly moved toward the Grandmaster. He snickered as they approached. "Lay a hand on me. See what happens. You know who I am. You know what I do. If not, your boss can tell you. He's my biggest fan. Touch me, and I'll put you in a hole so deep you'll never claw your way out. Hard labor every morning, cage fights every night. One hour of sleep if that. Bruised, bloodied, beaten, and not my problem. Or, better yet, I'll just melt you to death. Like a candle. Maybe in the morning when you first wake up. Is tomorrow good for you? I'm available all day." The four potbellied bodyguards backed away, hands in the air.

The Exalted Overseer stood up on his sofa so he was eye to eye with the Grandmaster. "I thought you were *so cool*, but you're just a joke. The people of Sakaar embarrassed you. I heard the story. They drove you away, and now you're running around like a desperate bug. Take a good look at me, cuz *I'm* the future and *you're* the past. Get out of here, you old weirdos. The Exalted Overseer has spoken."

The Collector rose from his seat, tossed his cloak over his shoulder, and took a moment to assess the situation. He was angry and frustrated that he'd been deceived. But the experience had a silver lining. At last he knew he had a bit of competition.

Thanos. All he had to do now was find him and destroy him. The thought made him tingle.

He tilted his head and addressed the Exalted Overseer in a low, soft tone. "We came here today to do business. I was under the impression you were a player, but your value, as it relates to the cosmos, is zero. You're a *nothing* who wishes to be a *something*. You play a child's game because you are a child. And I don't deal with children. I've seen and experienced things you only hear about in stories. I've held the Power Stone in my hands and lived to tell the tale. I've watched death and destruction rip apart the universe as if it were wet parchment. And yet, here I stand, undeterred from my mission. You don't have an Infinity Stone, and to stay here any longer would be a waste of my time; however, you have given me *some* renewed purpose. For that I'm grateful. But be aware, in the not-too-distant future, I will burn this establishment to the ground. Have a pleasant day."

The Collector sauntered confidently out of the room, followed by the Grandmaster, past the solitary hostess. "Buh-bye!" she chirped with a spritely wave. The brothers swung open the front door and exited onto the street.

"*That* was empowering," the Grandmaster said as they quickened their pace.

"*Move faster,*" the Collector said.

"We've been going all day! My feet are tired, and I need a massage," the Grandmaster complained. "Can we at least have *one* moment to relax and regroup? We need a new plan. That Infinity Stone is still out there! Don't you want to find it?"

"Of course I do! How dare you question it?!" the Collector shouted.

BOOM!

A fireball blasted through the front door of Cleeton's Retreat. The Exalted Overseer and his bodyguards ran out of the smoke-filled club, dazed and coughing.

"I may have stolen a small explosive device from Mizzala's collection and left it as a parting gift," the Collector said.

"I can see that," replied the Grandmaster. "Let's

return to the museum and formulate a new plan."

The brothers made their way down the street as quickly as possible, but the crowd was thick and getting thicker. It had become difficult to move. Revelers were littered everywhere. They danced and enjoyed the nightlife, paying little mind to the commotion coming from Cleeton's Retreat. Explosions were typical for a Friday night on Knowhere. The Collector tried squeezing through the mass of people, but a broad-shouldered creature covered in long, shaggy hair blocked his path. After unsuccessfully trying to push by him, the Grandmaster opted for a more direct approach. "Get out of the way, idiot!" he barked.

The beastly bystander turned around to greet the one person he'd come to Knowhere to find. "Well, ain't this a nice coincidence. Must be my lucky day," he growled.

"Nartaz!" the Grandmaster exclaimed. "How unexpected."

"You stiffed me on that hit job," Nartaz said. "I'm here to get what I'm owed."

"You said you didn't *know* a Nartaz," said the Collector, nudging his brother.

"I lied." The Grandmaster sighed. The brothers took off in the other direction, pushing people over to escape capture. They spotted an alley up ahead and struggled through the crowd to reach it. Nartaz was gaining on them. His plasma rifle was locked and loaded. The brothers turned a corner and slipped into an alley, where they found themselves confronted with a group of recent acquaintances: Yaan and the Cackalorns. They'd been drinking barrels of Flazen Milk and singing songs together since their dustup earlier in the evening. Upon seeing the Collector and the Grandmaster, their joy quickly shifted into anger.

"You!" Yaan shouted, pointing a beefy finger at the Grandmaster.

"Oi! Dat's da bum who wuz sittin' in your seat," said the Cackalorn leader.

"You're *friends* now?!" the Grandmaster barked. "I hate this stinking toilet planet!"

The brothers were trapped. Their enemies had

them outflanked. A few feet away, a deliveryman on a hoverbike prepared to take off. The Collector saw a chance to escape and rushed to take it. He moved toward the gentlemen slowly and carefully.

"Hey! The Collector! I know you," the deliveryman said, waving with delight.

The Grandmaster smacked him upside his head and clumsily pushed him off his hoverbike. "I would thank you, but, honestly, you should thank us," he said. "This is probably the most exciting thing that will ever happen to you. We're a big deal."

The brothers hopped on, held tight, and sped away to the museum.

CHAPTER 10

The Collector burst through the doors of his museum and dashed to his study as his brother followed behind. Their pursuers were closing in quickly, and time was of the essence.

"Release that—that cursed Xandarian Boulder-Crusher immediately!" the Grandmaster shouted. "We'll watch it feast."

The Collector's attention was focused elsewhere. "No, we won't," he murmured.

"Then what's the point of even having it?! You know, if I would've found a suitable bodyguard when I first arrived on this dump, we wouldn't be in this mess. This makes me almost miss Spord."

"Help me," the Collector said. He motioned to his chair.

"This is not the time for redecoration!" the Grandmaster exclaimed.

"PUSH!" shouted the Collector.

They grabbed hold of the large chair and moved it from its perch, revealing a hatch on the floor.

"Tell me this leads to a panic room," the Grandmaster said.

The hatch opened, and a cold iron pedestal rose from below. Sitting atop it was a lantern containing a glowing red mist. The Collector's most prized possession: *the Aether.* The Grandmaster couldn't believe his eyes. Before he had a chance to express his amazement, chaos erupted.

KA-THOOM!

Nartaz blew open the doors to the museum with his plasma rifle and casually strolled in, alongside Yaan and the Cackalorns. They'd bumped into one another when the Grandmaster and the Collector made their getaway. Realizing they were after the same two troublemakers, Nartaz invited Yaan and the Cackalorns along with him to track down their enemies together. "Where are you, Grandmaster?!" Nartaz called out. "I know you're in here. Come say hello to your friends." The Exalted Overseer entered soon after, covered in soot, carried on the shoulders of his four bodyguards. They all felt they'd been wronged and were itching for bloodshed. Not a single one was prepared to leave the museum without a fight. They moved into the main hall and came face-to-face with the Collector and the Grandmaster at last.

"You're *both* going down," snarled Nartaz.

The Collector calmly opened the Aether's containment device and released the pulsing dark matter into the atmosphere. Its hiss vibrated through the air. In seconds, the crimson fluid swept across the floor like a multiheaded serpent toward its prey.

The intruders froze in fear as the Aether's dark tendrils wrapped themselves around their bodies at lightning speed. "No! Please!" the Exalted Overseer shouted as it coiled around his bodyguards, strangling each one on its way to swallowing him whole. The black-and-red mass sucked every ounce of energy from his body, discarding the husk before moving on to its next set of victims. A whirlwind of darkness swarmed the Cackalorns, ripping apart their insides, one by one, until they all lay in a pile on the ground. Nartaz and Yaan fared no better. Their piercing screams echoed through the museum as the Aether morphed itself into a thousand small spikes and stabbed them. Repeatedly. Their life force sucked dry, their bodies dropped like a child's rag doll. The Grandmaster was mesmerized by the terror of the events he'd just witnessed. Having fulfilled its duty, the Aether returned to its containment device to hibernate until its next meal.

The brothers had defeated their enemies completely and were pleased.

"*SLAVE!*" the Collector shouted.

Keelan stayed in the shadows at first. She'd heard the commotion and hid to avoid the Aether's tendrils. The slaughter she'd just witnessed left her shaken.

The Grandmaster was breathless. "That was…

beautiful. And frightening," he said in an awed tone. "You had it. You really did have it all along."

"Of course I did. The Aether is one of the most powerful forces in existence. I don't leave it out for guests to gawk upon. It's not a conversation piece," the Collector scoffed. He grew annoyed. "*SLAVE!* Come in here now."

Keelan slowly moved out of the darkness so the Collector could see her.

"Clear these bodies," he said.

"No," Keelan said firmly.

The Collector was shocked by her response. "Excuse me?!" he bellowed.

Something had changed in Keelan. She was calmer than she'd ever been. It was as if a weight had been lifted from her shoulders. "Great and powerful Collector? You are nothing of the sort. While you napped and sulked, I watched your holovids and read your ledgers. I established trusted contacts. Made connections. You never suspected I could be so clever. You were too busy underestimating me to notice."

"Are you telling me your idiocy was simply an act? A smoke screen? I doubt it. You are a bumpkin, child. I gave you everything," the Collector said.

"You stole my life! I'm just *a thing* to you. I'm not a person; I'm part of your collection!" Keelan exclaimed. "You're a boy in a man's body, buying things because you're hollow inside. You gain strength by hurting others. But you won't hurt me. Not anymore."

The Collector motioned to the pile of bodies strewn about the museum. "You saw what I just did to these men and, yet, you persist?" he said, shaking his head.

"Petty little men and your cosmic games," Keelan spat. She reached into her waistband and retrieved a small, handheld cannon. It was an item the Collector recognized immediately.

"A Miniaturized Thermotron Collider," he said, surprise evident in his voice. "Where did you get that?"

Keelan smiled. "Pungo is like you. Desperate.

Willing to do anything if it means securing the thing he wants," she said. "I've been stealing items from the museum for weeks, pawning them in bits and pieces, saving up enough money so I could buy a weapon. It's not always easy to leave this place with you watching me, but I was relieved when you sent me on an errand earlier, to find the very Dotaki skull that I stole from you. It allowed me to retrieve this." She held up the weapon in defiance. "Your destruction."

"Pungo has deceived you about that weapon's capabilities." The Collector chuckled.

"No more lies!" Keelan shouted. She flipped a switch on the Miniaturized Thermotron Collider. It began to purr as she pointed it at the Collector. "You're cold and cruel and mean."

"I am all those things. Nothing you do will ever change that," the Collector said. "Put down the weapon, Carina. *Now*."

"My name!" she shouted. "Is Keelan!"

KA-THOOM!

As Keelan fired the Miniaturized Thermotron

Collider, the trigger malfunctioned, causing the weapon to backfire. The force of the blast violently knocked her into a tube of slugs. The tube's glass shattered instantly, covering her in slimy creatures. Dazed but unharmed, Keelan began to sob. After all her careful planning, she'd failed. Keelan trusted Pungo, and he had betrayed her just like everyone else. The realization left her devastated and embarrassed.

The Collector stared at her, weeping on the floor, covered in slugs, and felt a measure of sympathy. "It must've been difficult for you to come to Knowhere, all alone, without friends or family, to pursue a dream you had no idea how to achieve. I lifted you from the street. I gave you purpose. The nightly pain you must have endured, yearning for independence, unable to achieve such a thing. I cannot fathom it. Allow me to offer you an end to your suffering. Today, my dear, I will set you free." He grasped the Aether's casing and prepared to unleash it once more.

"*Wait,*" the Grandmaster said, raising his hand.

The Collector paused as his brother struggled to find the right words. "Clearly, I've been wrong about a few things. You had the Aether all along, which came in very handy. Thank you for saving our lives and all that. But, I wonder if, hear me out, you should let Keelan go. Were I in your position, I'd probably terminate her on the spot without a second thought. But! And I'm telling you something you already know, we are different people."

The Collector grew agitated. "Get. To. The. Point," he said through gritted teeth.

"Real power, true power, is hard to come by," the Grandmaster said. "I believe *mercy* is your best course of action."

"Hahahah! A *sociopathic tyrant* suggests I show mercy?" cackled the Collector.

"Is *that* how you see me?" asked his brother. "*Hmmmm*. It's not *untrue*. I do what I can to survive and make no excuses. But listen to me when I tell you this creature is no longer a threat. You robbed her of everything she could possibly use to hurt you. To destroy her now would only make you the thing she accused you of being: cruel, cold, mean. True or not, don't fulfill *her* prophecy. Then *she* wins. Tell me you see the sense in that."

The Collector considered his brother's words. He'd been obsessed with power for so long, he'd forgotten the many shapes it takes. Power isn't simply destruction. Power isn't always control. Power is building. Power is giving someone something you can easily take away. There was power in fear, and the Collector finally saw a new angle. He stared at Keelan unblinkingly. After a few silent moments, he reached into his pocket and tossed his hexagonal Memory Disk in her direction. Keelan caught it in midair and gripped the thing tightly, as if she were about to crush it.

"I wouldn't destroy that if I were you," warned the Collector. "There's information on it you'll find more than useful. I'm entrusting you with it. A parting gift."

"You think your stories and musings interest me?" Keelan spat.

"Child, they're not just *my* stories. They are the

stories of the universe. Answers to mysteries you didn't know existed. Be careful with that disk. Destroy it, and you'll never find out who ravaged your homeworld," he said. "It wasn't me, by the way."

"What should I do?" asked Keelan.

"Leave Knowhere. Never come back," said the Collector, throwing his cloak across his shoulder. "And be quick about it, Keelan. Before I change my mind."

Keelan rose to her feet, plucked a slug off her scalp, and tossed it at the Collector's feet. She smiled as she ran out of the museum. She was unsure of her future—all she knew was that she was no longer the property of a madman. That was all that mattered. She'd make up the rest as she went along.

"Feisty to the end. I like that," the Grandmaster said. "I wonder where she'll go, what she'll become. If Keelan had a bit of upper-body strength, I'd make her my new bodyguard."

"She's a survivor," said the Collector. "She'll become whatever she needs to be."

"I used to think you acquired things to make up for an ancient loss or some such, but that's not it, is it Tivan?" the Grandmaster said. "This isn't a manic hoard you've got here; it's an extension of *you*. The good, the bad, the excruciatingly ugly. What a strange little brain you have in that head of yours." The Grandmaster glanced at the bodies strewn about the museum. "Who's going to clean up this mess?" he asked. "You should hire that hostess from Cleeton's Retreat. She'll be looking for work."

The Collector released a long, exhausted sigh. "I should stop acquiring slaves," he said. "It's become much more trouble than it's worth."

"Would you stop using the *s* word?!" protested the Grandmaster. "And, perhaps, change your hiring practices." The Grandmaster spotted something on the Collector's workbench that he hadn't noticed when he first arrived. "Our old Astro Chips board," he said in amazement. "You still have it after all these years. Sentimental after all, eh?"

"I was in the midst of refurbishing the thing before I became *distracted*," the Collector said.

"Such a nostalgic fool." The Grandmaster grinned. "Let's play a game. To calm our nerves." He sat down and examined every inch of the Astro Chips board. "I hope you didn't rig it. I know how much you hate to lose. Oh! Do you have any Tesklazian tea? I'd like to draw a footbath before bed. And, to reiterate, I'm not sleeping on a cot in the basement next to the Xandarian Boulder-Crusher."

The Collector had grown tired of his brother's babbling. "Close your mouth for a moment," he said. "Our burden has lifted. Our enemies are vanquished. Let us enjoy this."

The Grandmaster looked around the museum, taking in his surroundings completely. It sparked a realization. "Who am I kidding? I can't stay here!" he exclaimed, launching himself from the workbench. "It just now hit me how hot and garbage-y this planetoid truly is. I'm over it. I need *relaxation*. I need *comfort*. I need *a firm exit strategy*." He squinted his eyes, lost in the thought of the moment. "Where can I find the Devil's Anus?"

"Excuse me?" questioned the Collector.

"Never mind. I'll find another way off this trash puddle," the Grandmaster said, marching toward the door. "Thanks for the hospitality. If one could call it that. See you 'round."

"That's *it*, brother? You sweep into my life in a flurry of melodrama and then leave once calm has been achieved?" The Collector scoffed. "Old habits die hard, I suppose."

"We had a laugh, Tivan. Don't spoil it with your gross sentimentality. You've got bigger things to think about," the Grandmaster said, pointing at the Aether. "Keep your eye on the prize. You didn't end up with another Infinity Stone this time around but I suppose the universe is young. At least you have the Aether. *For now*, at any rate."

The Collector grasped the Aether tightly. It was his most prized possession. He gazed at the crimson fury in his hands and felt it throb. When he closed his eyes and cleared his mind, he could hear the screams of his enemies. It was an energizing experience. At last, the Collector felt powerful and in control once again.

"What of Thanos?" the Grandmaster asked. "If he comes for you, it might not end well."

"Let him come for me. Let them *all* come for me," the Collector said, smiling at the Aether.

The Grandmaster stared at the shimmering singularity as its pulse slowed. "It's like a captive heart," he whispered in awe. "Why would the universe allow someone so *basic* and *unworthy* to possess something so incredible?"

"*Leave.* Your jealous stink is befouling my menagerie," the Collector stated.

"*My* jealous stink? *That's* rich coming from an obsessive troglodyte," the Grandmaster sneered. He stomped away in anger, pausing at the museum door to deliver a final message. Before he could open his mouth, the Collector delivered a message of his own.

"Whatever rude thing you're about to say will destroy any goodwill that's developed between us, En Dwi. Exit quietly. Do not seek my aid again. If you attempt to acquire the Infinity Stones out from under me, the carnage you've seen here today will become your fate," the Collector said calmly. *"Good-bye."*

The Grandmaster's eyes narrowed. "Good luck, Tivan," he said, dramatically throwing open his golden robe. "You'll need it." He stormed out of the museum, the door locking behind him.

Finally, the Collector thought. *I am without disturbance.* Ignoring the surrounding wreckage, he walked to his workbench, placed the Aether on its surface, and contemplated his next move. After a few moments of silence, a familiar thought crossed his mind. The Collector retrieved an unused Memory Disk and put the device in front of him. A wicked smirk formed on his face.

It was time to begin a new story.